House of Lads

ROLAND PARRY

First published in 2018 by Papalulo Press.

ISBN: 9781791543877

For Nancy and Eryl.

House of Lads

CHAPTER ONE

I got Ali every other weekend. When I turned up at theirs he'd be finishing his eggs. He'd put on that Minions cap I gave him and Leanne would fuss around getting him into his coat. She'd give me a look. She'd kiss him and wave him off.

I'd take him on the train to Southport or somewhere for the day. He'd stay the night at my bedsit in the top bunk. I'd play a bit of Battlefield and little Ali would watch and sometimes press the buttons. Till my Xbox got broke. So we'd watch telly instead. Sunday morning we'd have beans, then play in North Park if it was nice or go to the beach at Crosby. I'd drop him back round Leanne's at six. Not a minute later, unless I wanted a fight. Then back at work in the evening, zipping round on the bike with pizzas.

Some mornings I couldn't bear to crawl out of bed. But not them Saturdays when I had Ali.

So we were on the train home one Sunday afternoon and it pulled into Seaforth. I stared out at the blue cranes of the docks. The grey chutes of the corn mill. This bunch of lads got on and sat down a few rows away. Ali was standing looking out the window, making train noises. They couldn't see him. But me they caught looking. One of them yelled at me. Shaved-slaphead knob. All-white trackie.

"Fuck off, Paki," he said.

I looked away. Down. Breathed. Swallowed it. Tried to stop my heart pounding. Forced myself to sit still.

I started chattering to Ali. Tickled his stomach. Took his cap off and messed up his hair. That floppy black mop. I put his cap back on him. He chuckled. I tried to smile at him. Tried. He looked out the window.

"Stayshin!" he said. We were moving again.

"Yeah," I said. Tried to smile. Tugged the peak of his cap down. He chuckled and pulled it back up.

I kept still. Kept my eyes down, like I hadn't heard what the knobhead said.

They'd called me that at school. My dad was from

somewhere far away. Don't know where. But they could tell. We all looked the same to them knobs in Bootle.

They started skinning up spliffs, smoke rising as they warmed the resin. Screwing up the Rizlies and chucking them at each other.

I didn't look at them again. Kept still. Feeling the sting. Like at school when someone started on me. It never ended well.

Once some lad had caught me on a bad day. Called me it in the playground. I went after him. Got him in a headlock. Reached down with my thumb and finger and snapped his nose.

After that, they just called me Azo.

I tried to let it go. Held my breath till the next stop. The train doors hissed open. I stood up and led Ali off.

I sucked in my breath as the train pulled out with the bunch of lads on it.

Ali kept chattering away.

I stared across the track at the wet slate roofs of the terraces. I zipped my trackie top up as the rain started again. Ali was playing around. I chased him, held him still as he chugged and chuckled. Got his hood up and did his buttons.

We were only a mile from mine, but Leanne's house was all the way down the line so we had to wait for the next train. I sat there numbing my arse on the metal bench. Ali gurgling, pushing a make-believe car around on the seat next to me. I left him to it. Didn't feel like talking. That dickhead had set me off thinking the old thoughts, round and round.

They'd said my dad went away. Never told me where or why. When I was old enough to think about it, I guessed it was somewhere bad.

I didn't remember him much. Just a snapshot in my head. His black fringe and muzzy. We were leaning over a rail, flicking ice cream onto cars below. Southport pier, I think. I'd have been three or four. A single postie pic of him, trapped in my head forever.

I'd see him in my dreams and all, turning and grinning at me with his muzzy and three-stripe top. Cackling and chattering to us in some language.

I'd tried asking my mum about him. She never told me much. Looked at me with her soppy eyes and mumbled. This empty look on her face like she was soft in the head. Meeting me at the school gate. Spitting on her hankie to dab the gobstopper juice off my cheek. Chasing me and hitting me with her shoe.

She left me to myself a lot. Said she was looking for my dad. She never took us along. After a while I gave up asking. She stopped showing up at the school gate. Then one day I got home and her wardrobe was empty.

I shivered inside my trackie top. Rain and wind getting up. Lovely Liverpool summer.

Should've called Leanne and warned her we were late, but I had no minutes on my Nokia, did I. Nice one, Azo lad. Late for a meeting with Godzilla.

I got up and paced around to keep warm. Chased Ali up and down for a laugh. The train took half an hour to come, because it was Sunday. It sat stuck there for another half hour since the signals were messed up.

"Stayshin!"

When I got him back to hers it was quarter to eight.

I bent down and kissed him in the hall. Watched him vanish as Leanne sent him in the back. She had a right cob on. She rolled up the sleeves of her rugby shirt like she was going to hit me. Glanced at her watch. Gave me a look. Them burning blue eyes. Twitched her nose at me and folded her arms. Red freckles all down them. I'd liked that at first, when I'd met her that first summer. The older woman. That red hair. Not any more, eh. It was a danger sign now.

"His tea's well cold," she said.

"Put it in your Smeg cooker and heat it up then."

Let myself go for a sec there. Silly. I reined it in. Wished I'd hit that knobhead on the train now. Would have broken Frank's rule, but it would have made me feel better. I could have had him easy, the little scrote. Let some of the steam and noise out of my head. I couldn't let it out now. Had to be good with Leanne. She had strings she could pull.

Keep a tin lid on, I told myself. Breathe.

I said sorry. Didn't tell her about the train though. Didn't want to sound like I was wriggling. She'd not believe me anyway. So I didn't speak, did I. Should have. I bottled it up like always.

I waited for her to say something. I heard Ali in the living room, clattering the cases of his DVDs.

"If you're late with him again," she said, "I'll have to tell the woman."

It was the second time she'd said that.

Should have said something, shouldn't I. But talking never ended well. I couldn't keep my head and speak my mind at the same time. She'd talk the arse off me. She was smarter than I was.

I stood there in the hall, shuffling my feet and shrugging like a soft lad. She glanced at the wall next to me. Dent in the plaster where I'd punched it a couple of months back. I'd said sorry. I'd even said I'd grout it. She'd said no.

So now I was scaring her, eh. Frigging Hulk, me. Not like the cuddly little scally she'd hooked up with that summer at Frank's gym. On her settee after the Krazy House.

"There's that thing tomorrow at Saint Rock's," she said.

"I'll be there."

I stomped out the front door. Tried to slam it but it was one of them double-glazed ones with a rubber seal. It thudded and bounced back open. I grabbed the handle again and closed it slowly. I crunched over the stones down the garden path and whanged the metal gate shut behind me with a clatter. Crossed the road and headed for the train.

This old feller there, sitting at the bus stop across from her house. Short-arse. Skullcap on his head and one of them long white shirts coming down under his anorak. Grey beard.

He held my gaze as I went by. Smiling like he knew me.

Seen him before, I had. Couldn't remember where. He must have run one of the shops round ours. I wanted to ask him what he was looking at. Slowed my step and tried to stare him out. He kept smiling. I took my hand out of my pocket to give him the finger, but I stopped myself. Thought of what Frank would say.

I turned away. Put my hand back in my pocket and gripped my keys, my fist twitching. I wanted to punch something. Lamp post, car. Breathed deep and fought the feeling. Smothered it and stuffed it down inside me. I turned the corner by the Chinese chippy. Heard the old feller back at the bus stop blowing his nose.

The sting hadn't gone away, and it was worse now. It stayed with me all evening as I was taking people their pizzas. I ragged up and down on the bike at sixty, past the red-bricks on Linacre Lane. The gutted warehouses on Hawthorne Road. I took the Seaforth roundabout at forty, wobbling in the wake of the lorries as they pounded down to the docks.

I finished at midnight since it was quiet. Didn't want to go straight home on my own though. All that shit from the train and Leanne still boiling in my head.

I headed for The Grace to see if Frank was there. He'd spend his Sunday mornings at the ring training the lads, have a sleep in the afternoon then go down the pub in the evening. Bag of nuts. Pint of Cain's. His only vice, eh. That and his Bensons. It was where he'd always drunk after knocking off work at the docks, he told us. Before he got laid off and took over the gym. Before I was born.

I was passing the bus stop across from the pub when a 94 stopped at it. The doors opened and a feller got off.

The old beardy head from before.

Eh?

It was like he'd followed me. He saw me and gave me that smile again. Almost kind.

I stared back at him.

"What are you looking at, grandad?" I said.

He nodded and walked away. I let him walk. Frank would be inside. He'd talk me down.

I crossed over to The Grace. Its crumbling red bricks. Frosted windows. Peeling black paint on the door frame.

Frank wasn't there.

Hardly anyone was. A couple of scalls at a table in the corner. Trackies. Stoned. Laughing and pissing around. Gibby was always threatening to call the filth about lads like that. He bloody should have done. He should have done it before I showed up.

Gasping for a pint, I was. Worried about what Leanne said though. I needed to sort myself out. I'll not drink this week, I told myself. Swore it. Big try now. I sat on a stool at the bar, the far corner where Gibbsy had his old beer-towels all framed up on the wall. I asked him for a lemon squash.

"Where's Frank?" I said.

Gibbsy poured the squash in a pint glass. He looked at me over his shoulder. His red cheeks and thick square specs.

"One of his lads has got a fight on," he said.

Frank didn't have any kids. His lads were the ones at the ring. Big strip-lit gym in this cakey old brown-brick church off Stanley Road. I'd started going there when I was ten. Boss laugh it was. Twatting the bags and the balls. Stepping up and laying the other lads against the ropes. Frank taught us how to stand, breath, punch with all my weight. All my anger pumped into one blow. He tried to make sure I did it in the ring, not the playground. Tried. But the ring wasn't were I'd get shit about my dad. That was when the real twatting happened, eh. On the playground flagstones. Up against the glass of the bus stop. The grass and tarmac in the park.

Frank.

Most of the time he was at the ring. Two days after my mum fucked off, when the beans and Pot Noodles ran out, that's where I went. I was eleven. He took me to his. Made me fish fingers. I watched *Pop Idol* and slept on his couch.

After they put me in the home I'd still go to Frank's. The welfare spods had him on a list of good guys. I think he was the only one on it. He charmed the arse off my soshey worker. He was there for me all the way. Made sure I got through school. Taught me to drive in his old Cortina. Nagged me into passing my test. He was right. It's well paid for itself since.

All through my teens I'd drop by Frank's and hit the heavy bag. He'd spar with me, or hold the pads while I twatted them. He had this way of keeping your blood up while you were training.

"Come 'ead," he'd say, as you were punching the pads.

"Your mum hits better than that." You'd slam them harder. "Talking of your ma," he'd say then. "Tell her to pick her slippers up from mine." And so on, till you were bashing the pads like a sledgehammer to make Frank shut up.

I didn't take it to heart. I wasn't soft about my mum. For the kids at school it was more fun to skit me about my dad, whoever he was. They'd said it was the Iranian ice cream man who parked outside the school gate.

"Mr Whippy's yer dad," they'd sung. "Wanking in a Whippy wonderland." They're a poetic bunch of twats in Bootle.

When you were bamming the pads at full strength, Frank'd give up the smartarsing and just grunt along with every punch: "Your ma… y'ma… y'ma…"

Gibbsy put my lemon squash down on the towel. I picked it up and got off the stool. I needed a bit to myself. A comfy chair. I turned and headed for a table by the telly.

One of the scalls passed us on the way, going towards the bar. Black bags under his eyes. He wasn't even shaving yet. Yellowy skin and freckles.

He saw me staring. Growled at me as he passed.

"What yew looking at?" he said. "Yer fucking Paki knobhead."

A spark in my head like a wet leccy plug. Fizz and a pop. Bang.

I lobbed my pint glass.

Just meant to make him turn round, like. But it was one of those chunky ones with a handle. It didn't break. Brought him down with a big gash in his head. His trackie drenched in squash.

I waited for him to get up. He didn't. His mate had stood up though. I grabbed the empty mug and lashed it across the room at him. It broke that time. It smashed the mirror behind him with the Liver Bird painted on. The lad came at me anyway. He jumped over the table and ran in with his fists up.

I twatted him in the soft middle of his lips, the way Frank taught me. Felt my knuckle split on his front teeth. Then two quick jabs and I'd broken his nose. He went down.

7

I turned round to say sorry to Gibbsy, reaching for my wallet. Didn't get that far. A flash of yellow, and black, and I was face down on the floor. Handcuffs clicking in on my wrists behind. Blinding sting in the back of my head. Big hands gripped me under the pits, hoisted me up, turned me round.

A blur of black hats and neon yellow jackets. Pink mouths yelling in my face. A smell of leather gloves and truncheons.

Chapter Two

The cell stank of piss and cleaner. Grey-painted brick and a stainless steel bog on the wall. But the worst was the aching. I was all sore from being shoved around by the bizzies. My wrists raw from the cuffs, back bruised from being kneeled on. My cheek grazed by the floor of The Grace. You can act as tough as you like, but it's bloody awful, pain. It takes you over.

The light went off. I lay there on the mattress. Closed my eyes.

I slept. Then I heard the door clang.

I lifted my head. Someone had plonked a tray on the floor.

Breakfast. Muesli. Yuk. Runny fried egg on a plate with a placky spoon to eat it. Juice. At least that slipped down easy.

I sat there on the bed and drank it. Couldn't eat. Felt sick. I was lying on my side staring at the wall and thinking about Ali when a bizzie came in and told us someone had come.

He stepped into the cell and took his hat off. His old yellow BMX cap with the puffy square top.

Frank.

He sat down on the bed next to me. The strip lights turned his bald nut porridgy white. He didn't speak. Looked around him, his pale blue eyes glaring.

I tried to smile. Couldn't. Frank put his hand to the sides of his head and smoothed down the grey tufts. Hardly anything to smooth. He still didn't say nothing.

I'd let him down alright.

He waited. His old trick. Like a boxer, counting on me to throw the first punch.

"Did Gibbsy tell you what… "

He nodded. "Have they charged you?" he said.

"Dunno."

"You don't know if they've charged you?"

"They caught me with my cock out, didn't they."

9

"Have they let you see someone?"

"Yeah."

"Solicitor?"

"Yeah."

They'd grilled me as soon as they brought me in, after they went through my pockets.

"The rozzer wouldn't tell us fuck all," Frank said. "Just that the lad's in a bad way with his head split open. You should be seeing a judge this morning. Have they not said?"

I shrugged. There'd been all kinds of dickheads around the last night but it had been me doing the talking. I'd told them all what happened and they'd taped it. Not like I could hide anything.

I thought of Ali.

"How come they've let me see you in your cell?" he said. "They never do that."

I looked at him. He knew how things worked, Frank. I just let things happen. I'd thought he'd be giving us an earful. But he was quieter. He was looking well suss.

"What have they told you?" he said.

"Nothing. They asked me a load of stuff."

"What about?"

"All sorts. About my dad."

Frank rubbed his eyes with a finger and thumb. His lean old fingers. The tight pink flesh on his knuckles.

"Ten years ago, I was in this same building," he said. "Got to know all the bizzies here."

"How come?" I said. "Were you in trouble?"

"No, soft lad. I come here cos of you. When your mum left."

"Oh."

I got this sicky feeling in my belly whenever someone talked about my folks.

"They was trying to find out what happened to her," Frank said. "Me too. I helped them all I could. Then they just clammed up like they're doing now. Other bizzies, same shitty service. Perhaps if they'd helped you out then, you wouldn't be here now."

"So no one knew where she went?"

10

He sighed and reached inside his jacket. Got out his Bensons. Passed me one and lit it.

"The pigs knew something," he said. "They wouldn't tell us."

"That mean they knew about my dad as well?"

He sighed again. "Fuck knows."

"Do *you* know what happened to my dad?"

He put his head in his hands. Patted his bald nut with his fingertips.

"You ask me this all the time, lad. What do I always tell you?"

"Nothing."

"So what do you want me to say?"

"Don't know. Thought you might have found something out."

Frank spotted the tray with the egg. He went and picked it up and tapped his fag in it. Brought it back to the bed with him. Sat back down and looked at me.

"He call you a Paki?"

I nodded.

He turned towards us. Grabbed my head in both his hands, rubbing my cheeks, squishing them around like when I was a kid.

"I tried to keep you on the straight and narrow," he said. "I told you. Come any time and hit the bag. Hit the lads in the ring. Even hit me. Just don't hit strangers."

I wanted to cry. I held it in.

"I was looking for you, Frank," I said. "I was feeling bad. I couldn't find you."

"I was looking for you an' all," he said. "I called Leanne."

Frank didn't have a real phone. All his calls he made from the chunky old landline on his desk at the ring. And he never called me on mine. I'd told him to but he just didn't get it.

"I told her to tell you I'd be at the fight," he said. "Told her where you could meet us. Did she not say?"

I opened my mouth but nothing came out. Frank saw it on my face though.

"Don't be too harsh on her, lad. She's got a lot on her plate too."

I sniffed my snot up and looked at the floor.

"Does she know about this?"

He sighed. "Don't see why she would."

"Frank. I know I've let you down," I told him. "But you've got to do something for me."

He held the dish in one palm and ground his Benson out with the other. His knotty old knuckles turned white. I stubbed mine out too.

"You've got to go see Leanne," I said. "We're meant to be meeting with Ali's teacher this afternoon. Tell her I can't help it. Say someone jumped me and I'm being looking after."

"I can talk to her," he said. "She trusts me."

"Thanks Frank."

He got his Bensons out again and stared at the gold packet in his hand.

"But I'll not lie for you," he said. "You know that."

A bizzie opened the door.

Frank stayed where he was.

"On your way," the bizzie said. "And there's no smoking in here, thanks.".

Frank got up.

"You've got to look after Ali, Frank mate," I said. My voice sounded all small to me.

He put his cap on and zipped his jacket. Didn't speak.

"Can you drop by the pizza place?" I said. "They owe me two weeks' pay."

He stared at me, his old Paddy blue eyes all watery and sad.

The door clanged and he was gone.

Chapter Three

I woke up again. The door had clanged open.

I lifted my head and looked around, blinking. A bizzie came in with two chairs, scraping the legs on the floor. Another feller behind him. Tall. Suit and tie. Black briefcase.

I sat up and rubbed my eyes. My head throbbing and my belly all sicky. The bizzie went out, taking the tray. Another clang, and it was just me and the suit.

I looked at him.

Big clean-looking feller. He set the chairs up facing each other and pointed at one for me to sit.

I got up, still blinking in the light. Took a look at him. Some kind of bizzie? Not a boy in blue. This dark suit and tie. Lean, tough-looking bastard. Welfare? Army? Long arms and legs. Black hair, greying at the sides, swept back. Big posh straight nose.

He took the other chair, three feet away, and put his briefcase on the floor under it. He smiled at us. Big wide one. Like I'd said something funny.

"Hangover?" he said. This posh sneer in his voice.

"I wasn't drinking," I said.

"Muslim?"

"No."

"But you don't drink."

"Not last night."

That smile again.

"You fight though," he said.

I sighed and rubbed my eyes.

"I told them all this," I said. "They taped it. I had a bad day. Went the pub. He come at us. I decked him. I decked his mate."

He didn't look like he'd listened.

"So I spoke to the medics," he said. "That first lad. He's a junkie. Weak heart. Weak blood. Weak lungs. He shouldn't

13

have been picking fights with health like his. Well, anyway. He's dead."

I didn't get it at first. I looked up at him.

"Eh?"

"The lad you threw the glass at. He died."

"Eh?"

"Heart attack. On the spot there."

His voice was calm.

"How?" I said.

"You threw a glass at him, remember? Nasty heavy thing."

"But he can't…"

"He died, lad. You killed him."

I put my head down, elbows on knees, and hid my face. A teardrop broke on the concrete floor. Don't know why. I didn't feel like crying. Felt mad more than anything. I rubbed my head. Tiny bristles where Frank had clipped it a week before.

All I could think of was Ali.

I heard the scratch of a lighter. Saw his hand holding out a ciggie. Big strong fingers. Wedding ring.

Mister good rozzer, eh. Only he didn't look like any rozzer I'd ever seen. He looked like he knew what he was doing, for one thing. Like he was in charge. Must have been if he could get away with smoking in the cells.

I looked at him. He smiled and held the fag closer.

"Alright, lad," he said. He put a little foil ashtray by my feet. "Alright."

"Fuck off," I said. Tears in my voice, but soft, weary, like I didn't really mean it. I took the ciggie and sucked on it.

We sat there till I'd almost finished it and stopped crying.

"So you're Andrew Coke," he said at last.

I got my breath back. My lungs shuddered.

"Azo."

"Hello, Azo. I'm Paterson."

I sniffed.

"Where are you from, Azo?" he said.

"Bootle."

"Where further?"

"Don't know."

"Why?"

"My dad was from somewhere."

"What was his name?"

I ground the ciggie out in the little tray. Got up and had a wazz in the steel pisser. Acted like he'd not asked. Shook my knob off and put it back. Didn't care when a last bit drained down my leg and made spots on my trackies.

I sat down.

"His name?" he asked again.

"Don't know. He left, didn't he?"

"Don't you know where he went?"

I was too tired for all this. "Fuck off," I whispered. I started crying again.

He gave us another ciggie. I caught his eye as he lit it. Funny look in it. Almost friendly.

Something was going on.

"So where did your mum meet him?" he said.

He wasn't going away, this prick. I had to deal with him. I did like Frank taught us to do with bizzies. Big breath. Strength. Calm. Words.

"She was a nurse," I said. "In some war."

"And she brought him back here?"

"Don't know."

He stared at me, nodding. He reached down and picked up his briefcase. Laid it on his knees.

"You'll be looking at four years," he said. "You're twenty-four now. You'll not be the same after."

I put my head down again. Breathed deep and saw off the tears. I stared at the floor and mumbled back at him. "You walked in on me when I was having a wank just to tell me that?"

"I came to tell you there's another way."

"I didn't mean to do it."

"That may save you a few months, Azo. But that's not what I'm talking about. I'm talking about what you can do for me."

"Fuck off."

"Charming."

I sniffed and waited to see what he'd say next.

"How's Ali doing?"

Pigs always know that stuff. They'd have had it on file since that summer when they had us in. That night when it all went off in town. Trashing them shops. Nicking them saucepans. Boss laugh it was. The bizzies ran away. They caught us on some cam though, didn't they. Came for us at dawn.

I gazed at the floor.

"Poor little Ali," he said. "Seen him lately?"

"Fuck off. Who are you anyway? Where's your badge?"

His voice turned harder.

"I'm not a copper, Azo. I'm not talking about shaving months off your jail time. I'm talking about scratching it altogether."

I looked up at him.

"I could have your slate wiped clean," he said. "You'd get to see your boy much more. That woman you have to deal with, telling tales on you. I could make her stop."

I stared at him. I coughed.

He looked me in the eye. "By the way," he said. "They showed me the tapes tonight. From the pub. I liked the way you decked the second one."

"What do you care?"

He smiled. Winked. "You're a damn sight tidier than most of the scum that comes through here," he said. "Give me three months. I'll turn you into a deadly weapon."

I screwed my face up. "What you talking about?" I said.

"Don't you want to serve your country?"

"It's done fuck-all for me."

"Then young Ali will have to do without a dad."

He got up and straightened his jacket. Picked up his case and headed for the door.

"Have a good wank, Azo."

"Hang on."

He stopped as he was turning the handle. Looked back at us, raising his eyebrows.

"What is all this?" I said. "Help my country? I thought I was nicked?"

"A lot of my best chaps are." He winked. He walked back

over to us. "I like the way you fight," he said. "I like the way you look. You do what I say, lad, and I'll be signing papers."

"Then will I see Ali?"

"Right."

"When?"

"Never mind when, killer. The trick is that you'd get to see him at all."

He sat down again, put the briefcase on his knees and undid the clips.

"I want to see a lawyer," I said.

He clenched his teeth and whistled through them.

"I understand that, Azo," he said. He pulled a grey file out of his case and a pen from his jacket. "You're allowed one, too." He clicked his pen closed and open again. "But I can't let anyone see these papers. You want one, you can have one. But you'll do your four years. And you'll need more than a lawyer to see your boy again."

I sniffed in hard. A big greenie crackled up my nose and into my skull.

"How can I trust you?" I asked him.

"Who did you vote for last year?"

"Eh? No one."

"So you just let those fools in London run things." He pouted and made a joke of slapping his own wrist. "Mustn't talk about my bosses like that."

I stared at him.

He opened the file and passed it to me. "Read through as quick as you can," he said. "We've got a lot to get through."

He handed me the pen.

Chapter Four

I sat on the trolley with my top off and in came the doc. Bird in a white coat, open down the front. Tight wool sweater underneath. Reminded me of Ayisha Terni in fifth year. Clicking around in her sloppy twat on a bench behind the Glasshouse. I'd come a long way since then.

Paterson came in. He sat in a chair in the corner and opened a laptop.

They'd had me in at St. Anne's Street that first night but they'd moved me around in a truck since. I wasn't sure where I was now.

The doc strapped this rubber pouch round my arm, pumped it up and read the dial. Then a load of other stuff. Hit my knobbly knees with a hammer. Listened to my chest and back through a stethie as I breathed. Stuck a needle in and squeezed my arm so blood squirted in a tube.

"What's all this?" I said.

"Nothing to worry about," Paterson told me. "It's all in the papers you signed."

I never read them, did I.

Paterson looked at his files and hmm'd to himself.

"So it says here you like smoking cannabis." Eyes on his laptop. Screen shining on his face. "We'll flush all that out. Find out what other rubbish you've got floating around you. Work out what you'll be eating and drinking. You'll be a lot better once we get going." He winked at me. "You'll stop feeling bloody awful all the time."

They served me lunch in my room. Fish and mash and slimy spinach. I asked for ketchup but they'd not give it me. I felt knackered and sick. I only ate half the plate.

After the grub had gone down they took me to meet Ralph.

"Who?"

Paterson pushed open a swing door. I followed him through. Found myself in a gym. Backie-ball hoops. Lino floor. Mats laid out at one end.

He was standing there on the mats, stretching and moving his toes up and down. Ralph. Fifty-odd. Grey hair and beard. Square glasses. He looked like some sad old twat. Then he took his trackie top off. He was huge. Arms like rocks stuffed in a johnny.

He shook my hand. Crushed it. Said hello. Chirpy ex-para from Fazakerley.

Then he got to work.

My first lesson. He took a look at how I scrapped. Nodded when he saw all Frank had taught me. How to stand, how to breathe. We sparred a bit. He started weaving in all these fancy ducks and blocks. Wore me out. I lost my rag and tried to nut him. He dodged and swept my foot. Laid me on my back like a dickhead.

He gripped my wrist as he pulled me up. Then he showed me how to nut someone properly. Whole body zap, fizzing up from the heels, through his spine, balanced by his shoulders. Flashing out with a snap of the neck. Boss.

He freezed with his forehead an inch from mine.

"Bang," he said. "Your turn."

He kept me there two hours. Taught me four ways to kill someone with my bare hands.

Chapter Five

They'd moved me again in the night. When I woke up I was in some big posh jail. A room to myself. Long white lino corridors. Playing field, gyms, TV room. Even a pool table. Paterson and Ralph showed up too.

It went on for weeks.

Four hours each day with Ralph. Hand-to-hand. Then sticks. Knives. Bottles.

More. Outdoor cub-scout skills with a skinny old bloke called Jenks. First aid. Tracking. Map-reading. Where to point your compass, if you had one. Then street skills. How to break into stuff. Windows. Cars. I was all full of myself for having passed my driving test, but then they taught me to really drive. Taught me how to speed, how to spin. How to crash.

Bombs. Chems and plackys. Which wires to rip. Crapped myself a bit on that one. Not sure I'd remember all that techie shit. Paterson told me not to worry. Just base training, he said. I'd not need most of it since I'd be staying round Liverpool.

He got this Scottish bizzie called Kevin in to teach me about guns. Took a week. All kinds. More than I'd ever heard of. Baers and Brownings and Glocks and Grandpowers and Heckler and Kochs. Makarovs and Mannlichers and Mausers and Pauzas. Not to mention the shotguns and rifles. They made me learn the names. Sizes of slug. Weight. Pros and cons. Damage.

"You need to note this stuff when you see it," Paterson told me. "You need to tell me."

Kevin showed me how to put them together and shoot them. On a range, with earmuffs on like someone's gran. Boss laugh it was. Started with the handguns. Ended with an AK.

He set my hands and fingers on it, kicked my feet apart and squared my shoulders. I trained the sights at the paper figure and squeezed the trigger. Ding-dong. Kevo shouted well done, as I was blasting away.

Paterson'd pop in to watch me and make notes in his file. I was fucked if I knew where all this was leading, but I gave up asking.

Truth was I was liking it an' all. I was good at it. I frigged away at the trigger till my finger was sore, ripping them cardboard targets to bits. The pigs were well proud of me.

I didn't see much of the other lags, just passed them now and then. Skinheads, trackies, trainies. Footie shirts. Some looked like me. Some didn't. I'd stare as I went by them in the yard. Murder in their eyes.

Sometimes I spied the other lads through the gym doors, sparring alone against the staff. Ducking and kneeing and nutting. Cackling and loving it. Jogging up and down. Losing their rag and punching the walls. I'd look in for a couple of seconds before the bizzies hustled us on to another gym or the classroom.

That's right. It was back to school for Azo. They sat me down at a desk and had this spod called Lawrence in to talk to me. Young smartarse in a shirt and sleeveless sweater. He knew all about other countries. All these shitholes I'd never heard of. Full of scums who blew themselves up and kidnapped kids. All these gangs and networks and crappy little armies bumming each other in the desert. He made me learn all the names. Places. Leaders.

The fight training was boss but Lawro's lessons were a bunch of cack. He stood there slagging off all them dodgy countries. I wasn't fooled. I could tell those poor twats were just like me. He ran through the names of all these places and gangs and crap as if he knew it all. You don't live there, you bell-end, I thought. What do you know about it? And what do you care?

I got fed up after the first couple of classes. Didn't bother turning up for the next one. Found something better to do.

I'd made friends with another of the lads. Met him one day in the laundry room. Bungy. This chubby freckly lad from West Derby. He said they were flipping him to spy on some casino. He'd landed on his feet though, the fat sconehead. They wanted to plant him in a job in the kitchen there, so they were teaching him to cook.

That morning I skipped class, I ran into him coming out of the canteen. He'd been baking gingerbread and nicked a jar of nutmeg. He reckoned you could get high on it if you ate enough. He said it was the best buzz going.

I needed a laugh, didn't I. My head was too rammed with spy shit. I went out with Bungy and his jar, down to the yard and behind the shed where they kept the sports gear.

I karked down a mouthful of the spicy powder and waited for the buzz. Bungy snorted a big pinch of it straight up his nose and lay down on the gravel, oinking and turning red in the face. I pissed myself laughing. I couldn't feel the buzz yet but my belly was glowing and turning numb. I turned round and went to lean against the shed. Didn't make it.

Paterson was blocking my way.

"Lawrence is waiting for you," he said. "Why aren't you there?"

I shrugged.

"I asked you why you're not in class."

I told him the truth, eh. Thought he'd like that.

"I don't trust that spod," I said. "He's trying to brainwash me."

Paterson raised his eyebrows.

"He just wants us to hate foreigners," I went on. "So I'll go and twat them whenever you say."

"Perhaps you haven't been listening right. You've got to go to his classes. It's part of our deal."

"You've trained me up now. I could have anyone. I don't have to go back to school."

"Yes, you do."

He grabbed my arm and started tugging me away, aiming for the door across the yard. Two screws in their white shirts came out of it and started crossing towards us.

I shook my arm free. Paterson grabbed it again and shoved me against the wall of the shed, pinning me there by the shoulders.

"You're a tough lad, Azo," he said. "But you don't know whose side you're on."

"I'm not the only one."

"What?"

"I been watching the news."

It was true, God help me. They'd put a telly in my room but the only thing on it was the bloody BBC. All these kids dying from lurgy in Africa. Nurses and everyone catching it and spreading it around. Shit me up that. I'd never watched the news much. Now I remembered why. It put me well on edge.

"I've seen all the shit that goes on," I said to Paterson. "One day it's one country, next it's another. The same smartarses gobbing on about it. But no one's really got a clue what they're doing."

Fuck me. I really had been learning a thing or two. I was stringing whole lots of words together.

"You don't know where you come from, Azo," Paterson said. "You don't know who to fight for. Not yet. But we'll show you."

"What about that mess in Africa? There's thousands dead from that. Shouldn't we be building hossies there instead?"

He smiled. Smug bell-end.

"We will, Azo. Don't worry. We'll get there. Meanwhile we've got to take the fight to the bad guys elsewhere. That's where you come in."

"I'd be more worried about catching a lurgy and shitting myself to death than some lad with a rifle five thousand miles away."

He looked at me like I was nuts. "No one's going to give you a disease, Azo. You're letting yourself get stressed. Keep your mind on the job. There's always been diseases. But this other threat you're helping us fight, it's new."

I lost my rag. I knocked both his arms away and got one hand round his throat. This wicked neck grip that Ralph had shown us. It was Paterson's back against the wall now. I dug my thumb and finger in his throat. Any harder and he'd start choking. He knew it. He didn't wriggle. I kept my eyes fixed on his.

The screws had reached us. One of them went over to Bungy, took his jar of nutmeg and peeled him off the floor.

23

"Gerroff us," he moaned. "It's the best buzz goin'."

The other one came for me. Paterson raised a hand and held him off.

I eased my thumb and let him speak. He cleared his throat. His voice stayed calm.

"What's this really about, Azo?"

"It's been weeks. I've done everything you've said. I've not whinged. And you've not let me see my boy once. I don't have to put up with that."

He tilted his head, holding my gaze. He almost looked sorry.

"Yes, you do," he said.

"If you'll not let me see him, sod you. I've got no reason to stick around."

His gaze turned harder. "Then I'll give you one," he says. "I can pluck Ali off the street any time I want."

My voice trembled. "He's done nothing wrong," I said.

"True. He's a good lad, right?"

Tears pricked up under my lids.

"I've taken you off the radar," Paterson said. "I can do it to him too."

"He's four years old."

"They grow up so fast, don't they?"

Ten minutes later I was sitting in front of the white board, rubbing my eyes. Lawrence was teaching me all about the holy book. The nutmeg was kicking in.

The classes went on for days. Lawro told me tales and showed me snaps. Sick shit. Wars. Bombings. Stacks of corpses. They were messing with my head alright. I looked and nodded, but I didn't let them get inside me. I kept my mind on Ali.

I wasn't sure where we were, but the screws all seemed to be wools. Always the way, eh. They're in it together with all the rest. They'd keep all us Scousers locked up if they could. They took the piss out of me. Maybe it was part of the training. Called me a scally. They found out I was Evertonian and rubbed it in. Fucking glory-hunting Red wool mafia.

Sometimes Paterson sat in while they trained me, tapping away on his laptop. I sat tight and waited for the right time to ask him where I was heading. It was like Frank said. The bizzies knew everything. Even about my dad, maybe. But they'd not tell me for free.

Chapter Six

I looked out through the bars on my bedroom window. A car park and a patch of grass. I slurped the tea down. Got up and paced around my room. Nice big one with a thick carpet.

I felt boss. Fit. Strong. Alive. Hadn't had a drink my whole time there and I didn't want one. I felt like getting out on the mats with Ralph to see if I could take him down. Not that morning, though. I'd been called for. They led me down the hall with my trainies squeaking on the lino, over to the far wing where Paterson had his office.

He was sat at his desk looking at his laptop. Cardboard coffee cup. Waste paper bin. Grey steel filing boxes and a sofa. I sat on it and waited for him to speak.

He took a chewy out of his mouth, wrapped it in paper and dropped it in the bin. He gave me a smile.

"How are you feeling then?" he said.

"Shite."

He grinned. "You don't look it," he said.

He had this way of charming you. There was an edge to him though. I'd still no clue what made him tick.

"I told you we'd make you feel better," he said.

"You never warned me about Ralph. We were on the mats yesterday. He thought he'd make up some new rules. Almost bit my nose off."

"He's very pleased with you."

"That's a first."

Paterson's face went all blank. He did that a lot. Had a laugh, then dropped it fast and talked about something else.

"What did you think of all that stuff the spods taught you?" he said. He'd learnt that word off me. He had this way of using my words, even though it didn't suit him. "Those countries we're worried about. What do you make of them?"

"Sick," I said. "Evil." I'd learned that word off him.

"Yes," he said, softly. "It is." He nodded and stared down at

26

his desk. Then he perked up and looked me in the eye. "Azo. You told me when we first met that your father was from somewhere foreign."

I wriggled in my seat. That sicky feeling in my chest.

"That's what my mum said. I just remember him on Southport pier."

Paterson looked at his screen and nodded to himself.

"Do you think he was a good man, Azo?"

"No. He fucked off, didn't he?"

"Did your mum tell you why?"

I pointed at Paterson's laptop. "Doesn't it say in there?" I asked him. "It's got everything else about me."

He smiled and tapped the top of the screen. "Not everything. But I'll let you know if I work it out."

"Why are you so bothered about my dad anyway?"

"I want to know you better. Tell me, did the spods teach you what's going on in Syria?"

"Yeah. There's a bunch of scums and nonces who we're trying to batter."

He raised his eyebrows and looked at the ceiling while he thought that through. "Erm... yes. That's pretty much it," he said. He laughed to himself. "And what do you think of them? Those... *scums and nonces*?"

"Don't know," I said. "Guess if they've pissed the Yanks off they had it coming, eh?"

"So you think we're right to act there?"

I thought for a sec. "Me, I wouldn't go to all that bother just to kick some arse. But if you say they're that bad, then whatever."

I didn't know what I thought really. I'd say what I had to so I could get back to Ali and have a quiet life. But I didn't like the way this chat was leading.

"You think we're just there to kick their backsides?" Paterson said.

"That's what them drones are for, isn't it?"

"What about the people there, though?" Paterson said. "Aren't we helping them?"

"Rude not to, eh?"

He gave me that stern look. I was trying to be myself, but I wasn't being sharp enough for Paterson. I never knew how to play it with him.

"We're building a new future for that part of the world."

He made it sound like a shopping centre. I wondered if there'd be a Sports Direct. And a Costa. They've got boss flapjacks.

"Some people don't want us to," Paterson went on. "Even some people here in Britain. Even in Liverpool. They want things over there to stay the way they are so the scums can have their way. They say we are wicked. They brainwash young men like you to believe it. They use you to risk your lives for them."

Brainwashing, eh. Using me? That rang a bell. I didn't say anything.

"We've got to stop them, Azo," he went on. "So people over there, young folk just like you, can enjoy the same freedoms that you enjoy."

I almost pissed my kecks and cried at the same time. Freedom? My hairy arse. Follow the money. I held it in though. I'd taught myself to shut up and swallow all this cack.

"That's why I took you on, Azo," Paterson said. "You understand what's at stake for folk in that part of the world. You're one of the best chaps we can find to help them."

"I don't speak the lingo."

"Don't worry. You'll be staying in Liverpool where you're useful."

He winked and put his file on the table.

"Do you know Toxteth?" he asked.

"A bit."

"Know this newsagent's on Lodge Lane?"

He opened the file and took out a photo. Street view.

"No."

He'd written the address on the back. He showed it to me, then put the pic away.

"Well," he said. "You're going to get a job there."

That was a sick laugh an' all. I'd had a job before.

"They hiring?" I said.

He chuckled. "You could put it that way. But they're not the kind of folk to put an ad out. You'll have to go down and make friends with them."

"It's miles from mine," I said.

"You won't be at yours anymore. I can't have you living back in Bootle, with Frank popping round every five minutes. We've rented a flat in your name."

"And?"

"That's all for now. Here."

He reached in a drawer of his desk, took out a phone and handed it to me. My crappy old blue Nokia. With the buttons that hardly worked. I'd had it four years. Couldn't afford a new one. Hello. Someone had polished it.

"It looks pretty much like your old one," he said. "Works the same, but this one's in better nick. The phones are always a head-scratcher. It was too risky to give you a nice new one just for calling me. People would wonder how you got it. We can't have you going to calling booths all the time because you'll be seen coming and going and the lines are leaky. We can't afford to give you a year's stock of virgin SIM cards. In the end we've chosen this. You'll have to learn my number by heart."

He laid down a scrap of paper.

"That's how you get hold of me. Each time, as soon as we're done, you wipe the call memory. Remember that. Just this number. I'll always answer." He locked my gaze. "Any time of day or night, Azo. I'll pick up. You start talking and tell me what you've learned."

"And what am I meant to be learning?"

"We don't know."

"So I'm spying on this shop? Who owns it?"

"We don't know."

"I'll stick out like a sore arse just turning up there."

"Don't worry about that. Just be yourself."

"I'll have to make up a story."

"Just a bit," he said. "The beauty of you, Azo, is you're fresh and clean, ops-wise. We could dress one of our men like a scally but the scums would smell bizzie on him. You're a blank page. You could be one of those nutcases, or you could turn into one any time. So you're going to act like you're turning."

"Fun."

"You can tell them who you are. Your real name. You can talk like you, walk like you. Keep on bashing the bishop in the shower. You won't even have to mug up on Toxteth and make out you know it like you're from there. The whole story is that you're coming from a life spent in Bootle. The only bit you do have to think about is why you're moving."

I thought for a sec. "Have to be for work, wouldn't it?"

"Good. I think we're covered."

"Eh?"

"We went and told your pizza men what happened in The Grace."

"Why?"

"We said it was an assault, not a killing. Still enough for them to sack you on the spot."

"Thanks very much."

"You're welcome. Because now you've got good cause to be job-hunting. You're coming out of jail, and you've a big tatty-chip on your shoulder because you went down for a fight someone else started. And you're looking on the far side of the city, so you can stay away from the folks of the lad you battered."

"People get around."

"True. You'll want to watch out for them. But as far as a cover story goes, it's not half bad, because it's more than half-true. Rough bit of town, Tocky. You'll fit right in."

I sat with him for the rest of the afternoon while we padded out my backstory. Dab of bullshit here and there, polish it and paint it white. There was little enough of it, even a no-marks like me could make it sound real.

At five o'clock we had a break. Someone brought in tea and biscuits. When we'd finished, the door opened. Ralph came in with car keys in his hand.

"We'll drop you off just north of Smithdown Road," Paterson said. "You can wander down to your new flat. Get a feel for the place on the way."

This was it? Now?

"I need to get my head into this."

"Meh," Paterson honked. "Worst thing we can do is have you brooding on it."

He stood up and put his jacket on.

"Remember, Azo," Paterson said. "Don't try and see your boy. Or Frank. If you get in touch with them, your cover gets leaky. Then there's nothing I can do for you."

Chapter Seven

I walked along past the terraces with the bricks all painted over glossy red. Found a green door a few houses down off Lodge Lane. I unlocked it with the key they gave me. Walked up the staircase and let myself in. Put my rucksack down in the hall.

Bedroom. Living room. All clean. Carpet, telly. Little kitchen. Nescafe in the cupboard. Tins of soup. Bottle of lemon squash.

Someone had put up a high bar, wedged in the kitchen doorway. I jumped, grabbed it and did thirty chin-ups.

I went out again and walked up to the main road. A big greengrocer's on the corner with crates all laid out. Piles of these lumpy brown veggies I'd never seen before. I bought a banana and strolled along munching it. Hairdressers and cafes with all foreigny names. Bright pink and orange shop signs over the crumbling red bricks.

The newsagent was a hundred yards up on the left. I dropped the banana skin in a bin and looked in the window. Board with ads hanging there. I looked for a job going. Didn't see one. Just babysitters and odd-job men. Someone selling a guitar and amp.

A bell pinged on the door as I went inside.

A feller was standing at the till. I glanced at him and nodded as I passed. Didn't stare. Just a quick look at him. Glasses. Stubble.

I walked up and down the two aisles past shelves of bog roll and tins of beans. Took a can of Red Bull from one of the fridges. Looked at the magazines laid out across from the till.

I felt the feller watching me.

"You alright there, mate?" he said. English. Not Scouse though. Preston? Wigan? Them wools all sounded the same.

"Where's the paper with the jobs?"

"Out tomorrow," he said.

"I'd better come back then, then."

Clever, Az-lad. I knew this lot would be too dodgy to have an ad out. But I couldn't think of any better way to let on I was looking.

I was at the counter. He took my Red Bull and rang it through.

I got a closer look at him. Thirty-five. Balding. Spoddy with these round glasses and a cord jacket like a teacher. Scar on one eyebrow. Little pale circle, like a flap of skin got ripped off there.

He didn't want to talk. Mean frown on him and this hard stare through his lenses. He handed me the change and waited for me to leave. Didn't trust me. Didn't look like he trusted anyone.

I said bye to him as I went out the door. Well, that went well, spy lad. Same time tomorrow?

Someone told me the way to a gym down on Ullet Road. I smiled to myself when I walked past the road sign. Someone had spray-painted a B at the start.

I spent the rest of the afternoon there pumping away, thinking about the feller in the shop. Had to get him talking somehow. Get to know him. Catch his eye.

I had a Somali kebab for tea up by the Pivvy bingo. Went home and watched the news.

I headed back to the shop next morning. Skulked around a bit outside the window. Still no job ad. No one in there but the feller at the till.

I hung around a bit. Smoked a fag and pretended to listen to my voicemails. After half an hour these two lads showed up. About 16, in trackies.

I followed them into the shop. They nodded at the till feller and walked round to the far aisle. One of them picked up a golf mag and started showing it to his mate.

I went past them to the fridge in the corner, grabbed a can of Red Bull and took it back to the till. The feller had his eyes down on a newspaper.

"Alright, mate," I said.

He looked up.

"The jobs out today then?"

He pointed to where the papers and mags were. Far side, across the second aisle. Two lines of shelves in between. I could see the tops of the two lads' heads.

I went round and stood in the aisle beside them. I moved quietly. They didn't spot me. As I bent down to pick up the paper, I looked across at the one with the mag.

"What you got there, lad?" I said.

He shrugged and showed me the cover.

"Yeah, I can see what it is," I said, louder. "Why was you putting it in your jacket?"

"You what?"

"You heard. Who do you think you're stealing from?"

He turned red.

I looked over my shoulder to see what the feller at the till was doing. He'd not said nothing. Not moved. He wasn't even looking at the lads. He was looking straight at me.

The lad's mate piped up. "Leave him," he said. "He wasn't doing nothing."

"Not what I saw."

He wasn't scared, the mate. Not yet. He turned to the other one and muttered something. They both smirked.

I barged towards him. "What did you call me then?"

"Nothing."

"You call me a Paki?"

I was getting close to him, staring him out. He muttered again.

"You what?"

He raised his voice this time. "I never!"

"What's your name?" I said. "Both of you?"

"You knob," the mate said.

I had the paper rolled up in one fist. I raised it like I'd hit him with it. They scuttled down the aisle towards the back. I ran after them, round the corner and back down the middle as they went crashing out the door.

I yelled and kicked it shut behind them.

The feller at the till was still staring at me. I handed him the paper and reached in my pocket for change.

"Sorry mate," I said.

"Welcome to Toxteth."

"You get that all the time?"

"They trashed the place a few summers back. Crowds of buggers like him."

"What did they do?" I said.

"Broke stuff. Nicked stuff."

I didn't tell him I'd been out them nights too, robbing myself some cooking pans.

"They hate us, don't they?" I said. "That's why I lost my job."

He put my paper and can in a placky bag together. I pulled the paper out again and leafed through it.

"I heard there'd be jobs round here," I said. "How much do you get for walking some old lady's dog?"

He was quiet for a bit. Then he spoke.

"Can you drive?"

"Yeah. I can ride a scooter an' all."

"You're fancy, you, aren't you?"

"I went to a posh school."

He smirked at that, just for a sec. I opened the Red Bull and slurped half down.

"Why do you ask if I can drive?"

He didn't answer. I stuck my hand out. "Azo."

He didn't shake it. He stared at me, then said: "Mossie."

"Where you from, Mossie?"

He gave me this suss look. Wondering what I was after. I'd gone in too hard.

"Sorry, Mossie, mate," I said. "I'm a nosy twat. As you saw." I looked over at the magazine rack where the lads had been.

I opened the door and headed out, pinging the bell. I walked to the corner and looked back at the shop. Two floors. A window on the upper one.

A light was on behind the curtain. I stood staring at it. A hand twitched the curtain and a chink opened at the side. I strained my eyes to try and make out a face. Couldn't. Just a set of big pink knuckles.

Chapter Eight

I kept working out at that gym. Talked to anyone around Toxteth who'd listen. Padded out my hard luck story, hoping some of it would drip back through to Mossie when people came in the shop. I helped folks out with odd jobs. Carried shopping for mums. I bought kebabs and cups of tea up and down Lodge Lane and had my head shaved in the Yemeni barbers, gobbing away the whole time.

I popped into the shop every morning that week for Red Bull. Tried to get Mossie talking, but he was hard work, that lad.

"You sure you're right about this bunch?" I said to Paterson on the phone. "He asked me if I could drive. But he's not acting like they want to hire anyone."

"Trust me, lad," Paterson said. "They're just looking for the right man. An angry young one like you."

"They're taking their time."

I snooped around the shop as much as I could. The upper windows stayed curtained. The back door was in a yard behind a locked gate and a wall with broken glass on top. I'd watch Mossie closing up and opening. He'd talk to the greengrocer and the man in the phone store. I chatted with them too and made sure they remembered me. Mossie drove this red Honda to and from the shop. I didn't have any wheels myself so I couldn't follow him home. Didn't dare ask one of the fellers from the cab firm in case word got back to Mossie. So I just called Paterson and passed on the car reg number.

I was running out of chatter to try on Mossie. I lost sleep worrying I'd smegged up my chances by being too nosy that first day. Nothing for it though. I kept popping in. By the seventh day my banter had dried right up. I'd have to sit off and think about how to play it with him. I picked up my Red Bull from the counter and was turning for the door when he spoke.

"Where you from?

"Eh? Bootle."

"Where further?"

"Why?"

He didn't answer.

I sighed. "My dad fucked off, didn't he."

"Four fifty an hour," he said.

"Eh?"

"He's told me to offer you a job."

"Who?"

"Boss."

"Why?"

Mustn't look too keen, like.

"Had a better offer?" he said.

"Fuck off."

"The boss might ask you to do odd jobs for him. He pays overtime."

"Is he queer?"

"Better not let him hear you say that."

"'Cos for four fifty an hour, he can suck my knob."

"He'll come down and wash your mouth out for nothing."

"He can try."

He gave me that quick smirk. "I told him about you, Azo. He liked the sound of you. Said to give you a chance."

"Does he want to see my CV?"

"No. Just one thing. Did you vote?"

Second time in my life I'd been asked that.

"When?"

"Ever."

"No."

"Good."

"Why?"

"Because you can't let people run things, Azo. They're too thick and greedy."

"I agree with that."

"Good. Only God can run things. If people get in his way, you have to stop them."

"How do you do that?"

He came out from behind the till with something in his hand. A Stanley knife. He held it out to me.

"You'll not find any other jobs round here," he said.

He took me in the back, through a doorway hung with long placky ribbons, into a dingy old hallway. Boxes of Monster Munch, floor to ceiling. Red ones and purple ones. A patch of green carpet and a back door. He pointed at the boxes. Told me to slash them open and lay out the packets on the shelves.

I tried to hide how made up I was. Paterson would cream himself.

Steady, Azo, lad. One step at a time.

I took a stack of boxes through to the shop. Looked at the placky knife in my hand. I switched out the blade.

I called to Mossie. "Does this mean I have to start praying too?"

"Are you a believer, Azo?"

"My mum was. Maybe my dad was. Me, I don't know what I am."

"Maybe here you will find out."

Chapter Nine

I was a boss shelf-stacker, me. Monster Munch. Skittles. Jars of Marmite. You should have seen me line up them Scotch eggs in the cold bit.

It didn't feel like being a spy.

Bit by bit Mossie started looking more me in the eye. He told me he was from Wigan. I wasn't getting any juicy leads from him though. And no sign of the beast in the attic. Mossie wouldn't let me go up to see him. Wouldn't tell me nothing about him. Not even his name. Told me the boss would come and say hello if he wanted. When he wanted.

"Trust me, lad," Paterson said. It was two weeks after I'd started. "They're just checking you out. They've got to be careful who they let in."

"They don't seem very sure about me."

"Perhaps you're not being evil enough."

Another week later I was on my knees stacking tins of oxtail soup, still thinking about that. I heard a voice.

"'Ey. 'Ey, lad."

I turned and stood up.

Lad my age but taller. Lanky, white. He was standing facing me with his back to the till. Mossie was watching.

I cacked myself. I'd been waiting for this. For that lad from The Grace to track us down. The one I didn't kill. This wasn't him, though. One of his mates, eh.

He came up to me dead close, looking down in my face.

"Did you start on my little bro'?" he said.

"You what?" I said.

"He wasn't doing nothing."

I felt better already. It wasn't about The Grace. Just the lad with the golf mag. All my chirping around had got me known. He'd worked out where to find me. It had taken him a month to track me back to the same shop where the whole thing started. He was hardworking, this lad, as well as clever.

Out the corner of my eye I saw Mossie look up, all grumpy. I'd better see to this quickly.

"Fuck off," I said to the lad.

"Come 'ead then." He shoved me. I fell sideways, knocking tins on the floor.

Nice one. Just when I thought things were starting to thaw with Mossie, now I'd be trashing his shop in a scrap with some scrote.

No choice though, eh. I steadied up, balanced, breathing. Ready.

"He's a thieving racist little knobcheese," I said.

The lad shoved me again. "He's fifteen. How fucking old are you?"

I stood on tiptoes and put my face right up to his.

"Fuck *well* off."

He shoved me a third time. "Come 'ead then, I said."

I glimpsed Mossie reaching over the till to the door. Turning the sign round to Closed.

I slapped at the lad. Wound him up. Called his mum a slag. Always worked. He swung at me.

I caught his wrist and twisted it behind him the way Ralph taught me. So he couldn't move an inch without feeling like it would snap. Shoved him to the floor face first and sat on him. He lay there breathing deep through his nose, taking it without a word. I rubbed his face around on the lino. Old chewies there, stamped in.

I got my free hand to his neck and pressed my thumb on the spot Ralph showed me that first day. All the squishy, crunchy bits of flesh and windpipe. He stopped groaning and went quiet.

I held him steady and glanced up at the till. Mossie was leaning over to look. Calm. Well into it.

I squeezed harder with my thumb. The lad gurgled.

"What's that, lad?" I said. "Can't hear you!"

He spluttered and growled.

Harder.

He was going purple, hitting the floor with his palm. I turned my head and smiled up at Mossie. Squeezed harder again.

Mossie piped up. "Come off it Azo, lad. You're going to kill him."

"Kill him? Now there's a thought."

Mossie frowned.

My mad act now. I screwed up my face. Spit flying as I yelled. "And what's anyone going to do about it? Slag us off till he comes alive again?"

I eased off a tad. Heard snatches of air in and out of the lad's throat. I squeezed it again. He gripped my arm, trying to tug it off him. His fingers turned white and slipped away. I bashed his head against the floor, printing a red mark all down his cheek.

I let go and got up off him.

He rolled away, wheezing. I grabbed the waist band of his trackies. Shiny cloth tore under my nails. I peeled them off, tugging hard to get them over his trainies. He twisted and flipped about on the ground in his boxies. I balled the trackies up in my fists and chucked them at him.

"Come 'ead then," I said.

He crawled away half naked, coughing and spitting, towards the door.

I'd made myself some enemies in Toxteth, then. Bit much, using my training to batter some poor scrote. I was meant to be watching over my fellow countrymen. That's what Paterson said spies were for. I had to know whose side I was on, he'd said. He was good at messing with my head.

The door rang and rattled shut as the lad slipped out. Then another noise came from the back of the shop. Rustling of the ribbons. I looked over. Saw his back as he passed through to the stock room. A big feller in a blue vest.

He'd been stood there. Watching.

Mossie stepped from behind the till. He left the *Closed* sign facing out.

"The boss," he told me.

"He'll have it in for me then."

Mossie smirked. "I think he likes you." He patted my shoulder. "If you see any more little bell-ends thieving," he said, "you know what to do."

41

"Welcome to Toxteth, eh?"

"Ay. A godless place in a godless land. Just the homeland they deserve."

"Eh?"

"The British," Mossie said. "For carving up our lands and leaving them in pieces. You should know all about that."

I didn't know what to say. Felt his stare on me. He meant it. And he wasn't done.

"The souls of the dead from their murderous empire are coming back to haunt them. They will not be put to rest."

Fuck me. Who was this spod? He'd got well wet from seeing me scrapping. I tried kissing his arse a bit, to see if he'd loosen up some more.

"You sure you're a wool?" I said. "You sound well too clever."

"My forefathers were from Syria."

A noise came from upstairs. Footsteps crunching back and forth. Someone yawning and clearing his throat. I stood up and went in the back for some jars of pickle. This narrow staircase there, leading up between two stacks of boxes.

At the top of the stairs, the door opened.

Chapter Ten

He came crunching down the steps.

It was gloomy in the back there. I couldn't see his face. He found a space between two stacks of boxes and squatted on his heels with his back to the wall. Nimble move for such a big twat. His knees didn't seem to give him any gyp.

He waved for me to sit. I sank to the carpet and rested my shoulders against the wall.

He cracked the knuckles of each hand and rested his elbows on his thighs.

He had this baggy vest on. Tattoos all down both arms. Old black ink turning blue and green. All kinds of cheesy shit. Anchors, mermaids, treasure chests. Welsh dragon. Irish harp. Liver Bird.

Big, he was. But not a fat knacker. Tall and thick in the arms and legs. Barrel chest. Knuckles. I couldn't see his face yet, just this old green baseball cap on his head. Peak down, eyes on his lap. He reached up and plucked it off with two meaty fingers.

I got a good look at him now.

These light green eyes, huge and wide with tiny pupils, like a stoned cat.

Where was he from? Couldn't tell much by looking. Dark red face, sunburnt and weathered. Chunky forehead. Shiny red cheeks. Big mouth with one tooth sticking out skewiff. Hair on his head browny red and clipped close. Shine of grey at the temples. Straggly ginger whiskers on his chin.

He must have been at least fifty, but he dressed like he was half that. Baggy combats, trainers, blue Adidas vest. Two rings in each ear. Black placky digital watch.

He held his cap in one hand and flicked it against the palm of the other. Looked at me with those misty green eyes. They didn't move together. Didn't quite point the same way. The left one had a lumpy scar by it. I tried to look at him in that

43

one, but kept switching.

He smiled again.

"Azo mate," he said. "I been looking forward to meet you."

Scouse in his voice, but there was more to it. Like he wasn't from Liverpool in the first place. Or was, but he'd been away so long he'd forgot how to talk.

"I'm Raz," he said. "Your boss."

He held out a hand.

I got up, leaned over and shook it. He crushed my fingers in his rough palm.

"Sorry about the fight," I said.

"Mossie told me you had a hard time. Lost your job, eh?"

"Yeah."

"You a good lad, eh? Live with your mum and dad?"

"No chance."

"You got kids? Wife? Bird?"

I thought of Ali. Felt a squirt of sadness in my chest. Tears under my lids.

"I got nothing."

Paterson had told me I had to be a good actor. I hardly needed to act when it came to telling Raz my sob story. I looked him in his lazy eye and let it all gush out. My mum, the home. Frank and his boxing ring. Learning to fight. Fighting. Getting in shit.

I didn't tell him about Leanne and Ali, but all that other stuff was enough to be getting on with. I clenched my fists and fought back the tears. I'd worried about not doing a good job of bullshitting like this, but a funny thing happened. It felt real.

Raz reached down beside him and bashed a fist through the top of one of the boxes. He rustled around and brought out a bag of Monster Munch. Ripped it open and stuffed a fistful of the crispy chunks in his gob.

He narrowed his eyes as he was chewing. Peered right at me. "What about your dad?" he said.

Again, no acting needed.

"Never met him, Raz mate," I said.

He looked me in the eye. "Wish you had?" he said.

"Yeah. Wish I could meet him now. I'd rip his knob off."

I held his gaze as he gobbled the crisps. He spoke again through a sticky gobful of splodge.

"So you never knew who you really was, or where you was from."

"Yeah I do. I'm Azo Coke. I'm a Scouser."

"Aren't we all, la'. But you feel like you got no dad. No home."

I kept my act up. Fixed this look on my face, like I hated everything. Like I wanted to tear it down. I said it again and meant it.

"I got nothing."

That's what he was after. He swallowed the last of the Monster Munch, blew up the bag and popped it.

"That's good," he said. Then twisted his face into a smile. "I mean, what's good is you got a fresh start now, eh?"

"Have I?"

"You like working here?"

"Don't know. Just started."

"Where did you work last?"

"Pepper Pizzas off Scottie Road."

"What happened?"

"I went down, didn't I. For duffing up some racist shit."

Raz raised his chin. His green eyes caught the light.

"What he say to you?" he asked.

"Same old. Go back where I came from."

He nodded slowly. Blinked. His tongue lashed out sideways at a scrap of crisp in his beard.

"And how'd that make you feel?" he said.

"Fuck off."

"Come' ead, Azo lad. You can talk to me. When they said that. How'd it feel?"

I kicked my heels and played it all angry.

"Wanted to pan his head in, didn't I. I did, didn't I."

Raz smiled to himself. He clasped his fists in a mace like he was praying. He was quiet for a bit.

"I know a lot of lads like you," he said at last. "Jumped. Fired. Dicked on. Want to fight all the time. I understand that. Stick with me, la'. I'm going to help you."

"I'm not some div who needs help."

"Well maybe I need your help too."

I nodded towards the front where Mossie was at the till. "He doesn't like me. I'm not a believer."

He shrugged. "Me neither."

"Why's Mossie here then?"

"He needs hard-knocks like you and me, la'. He'd not get far on his own."

"But we're not believers, are we?"

He sniggered. His sloppy toothy gob. His eyes sparkled.

"Speak for yourself, la'. I believe in lots of things. Stick with me. I'll make you believe them too."

I frowned at him. "Why do you want to help me?"

His twisted smile. "I like you, Azo," he said. "Thirty years ago I was sitting where you are now. Lost. Angry."

"How did you sort yourself out?"

He leaned forward, straightened his knees and stood up. "Went on a journey, la'. Learned to fight. Learned to think. Grew clever. Grew strong. Came back. Never the same."

He opened his fist and let the screwed-up crisp bag fall to the carpet. He stuffed a hand in his pocket, brought out car keys and dropped them in my lap.

Chapter Eleven

"So you're his driver now?" Paterson said.

Midnight. I was in bed in my flat, under the blanket, holding the Nokia to my ear.

"He lost an eye. He needs someone to drive him."

"Keep talking."

I told him all about my day. I'd spent hours in Raz's old white Astra. Drove him out to Warrington and sat at the wheel waiting while he called in on "friends". Raz hadn't told me what he was up to. Looked like nothing to do with the shop. I didn't ask. Didn't say nothing. Just fixed it all in my head till I could call Paterson. He lapped it up.

He wanted to know all about Raz. Where he went, when. Street names. Times. Was he armed? Not that I could tell.

"Well, keep an eye out," Paterson said. "He will be."

I gave him the number of the Astra.

"Thank you, squire," he said when he'd noted it. "And well done on your backstory. Your man Mossie dropped by the old pizza place to check out if it was true. Seems it all stood up."

"Mossie went there? How do you know?"

"A little pigeon cooed it into my ear."

"Oh aye. Got a lot of them, have you?"

"All over town, though you wouldn't know them. Don't be jealous, Azo. That's how this works."

"So you've got a whole little slave army of twats like me?"

"There's no one quite like you, Azo."

I sighed. "So where's all this leading?"

"If I knew that, I wouldn't need you."

"Can I see my boy?"

"You know the rules, lad. Stay where you are. Keep your eye on Raz. And stay in touch."

I couldn't stop thinking of Ali. I missed kicking the ball with him in North Park. Taking him to his swimming class. Every time I asked Paterson about seeing him, he farted us around.

Raz had said I could have Sunday off. That was Ali's swimming day.

Chapter Twelve

I got to the baths at quarter to eleven. Used to take Ali there myself. I'd stand in the water with him as he chugged around in his armbands. We'd sit at the poolside after and eat Nik-Naks from the machine.

I didn't have a plan for when he and his mum came out. Wasn't safe to go near Leanne. She might call the filth.

One thing I was even more scared of though. Seeing Ali. Scared he'd not remember his dad. Or he would, and he'd hate me. All those weeks away. God knew what she'd been filling his head with. I wondered if anyone had told him I was a killer. Wondered what a three-year-old kid would make of that.

There was a patch of grass round the side of the pool building. Couple of swings. I sat on one of them and lit a fag. Held the chain in one hand and smoked with the other. Kicked myself back and forth, keeping an eye on the path to the front gate. If anyone came out of the baths, I'd see them from behind.

I could hear the shrieks and splashes from inside the pool. The next class had started. Ali would be done.

Another ciggie to calm me down. I was grinding it out in the grass when people started coming out. Mums and dads and kids in pushchairs. Down the path and through the gate they went, peeling off left and right and lining up at the bus stop.

At last I saw him. Running down the path, fanning his coat out behind him like Batman.

I held my breath, waiting for Leanne to come out. But she never did. Someone else came instead. A taller figure walked slowly along the path and caught up with Ali at the gate.

I swore softly to myself, with a big grin on my face. I saw the old blue anorak and yellow BMX cap.

Frank.

He never let me down, the soppy old twat. What would he

49

say to me now, though? What would he do? Last time I saw him he was turning his back on me in that cell. I was wary of him now. You could never take him for granted. Frank and his code.

I hopped off the swing and followed them out the gate. Got to a few yards behind them, staring at the back of Frank's anorak. His arm round Ali's shoulder.

They stopped at the bus shelter and sat on the bench to wait.

I walked up to them. Frank was sitting, pretending to steal Ali's nose. Ali was jumping up and down and laughing. They'd not looked my way yet.

I stood right by them and watched. My hands in my trackie pockets. Knot in my chest.

Time went slow for a second.

"Alright Frank," I said. "Alright Ali, lad."

Ali looked up at me and smiled. Shy. At least he remembered me. Least he wasn't running away.

I met Frank's eye.

He looked me up and down. Took his cap off and smoothed his tufts of hair. Looked me in the eye again and nodded.

I squatted down next to Ali.

"What you been doing lad?" I said. "Been swimming?"

He nodded quickly, smiled shyly. Looked the other way.

"Did this old knobhead buy you crisps?" I said, pointing at Frank. "Or shall we beat him up and take his money?"

I ruffled Ali's hair and pulled his hood down. He gave a gurgly laugh.

"Come 'ead," I said. "Let's do it." I stooped and tickled his tummy.

Ali chuckled and shook me off.

"We 'ad Nik-Naks," he said.

"Well thank God for that." I tickled him harder. "You going to give us a hug then?"

He put his arms round my neck. I wrapped my arms about him, lifted him off the bench and stood there squeezing. The sound of his breath. Clean bleachy smell of him. His wet hair on my cheek. Relief, plus something else. Happiness. Sadness. Don't know. It felt boss.

I sat down beside Frank. Held Ali on my knee and tickled him again. He couldn't stop laughing now. We watched their bus come and go.

Frank looked at me. Still suss. Waiting, like he did.

"Can't stay long, Frank," I said. "Got to keep my head down."

"You on the run now?"

"Nah. I'm alright. But they don't let me out much."

"They let you out today. Whoever they are."

"Day off."

This miffed look on his face. "Day off from what?" he said. "You working?"

I'd never thought of it like that. "Yeah," I said.

He kept his eyes fixed on me. "And?"

I lit another fag and handed one to Frank with the lighter. I'd known it was going to be tricky. But I owed Frank something. He'd kept up his side. He'd looked after Ali. Made sure I wasn't forgotten. I was there now, wasn't I. I'd broken Paterson's rules already.

I took a big drag. "I'm working for the pigs," I tell him. "I'm a grass."

"You blagging me?"

"No."

Frank frowned. "On who?" he said. "You don't know anyone worth grassing."

I'd told Frank more than I should.

"Come 'ead," he said. "Who?"

"Don't ask. You'll get me in trouble."

"Oh, right, yeah. Trouble."

He glared at me.

"Are you on drugs?" he said.

"Fuck off."

I gave him my bicep to feel. I put Ali down, leapt up and did five chin-ups, hanging from the bus stop roof. Ali liked that. Wanted to do some himself. I lifted him up to the roof and helped him try. Grunting and chuckling, the two of us. Then I panicked, afraid someone'd see me. I put him down and we sat back on the bench.

51

Frank sat there, thinking. Bee in his bonnet.

"Alright, Usain Bolt," he said. "No drugs. What then?"

"Told you. I'm working for the pigs. Undercover."

"So which rozzer you grassing to? Mather? Dyson?"

"You don't know him."

"Don't tell me it's counter-terror."

"Can't tell you no more, Frank mate," I said, and slapped him on the shoulder. "I'd have to kill you."

He shrugged again and puffed his ciggie. "Least you've not lost your balls."

Ali was standing in front of me, punching my knees. I grabbed him and hugged him to me.

We watched another bus come and go. Ali started play-fighting, hopping about and cuffing me in the kidneys. Frank leaned in and fixed his stance. Showed him how to balance and jab. Ali tried it on me but I tickled him till he gave in. I handed him the Nokia to play with but he didn't want it. He was too used to his mum's smartphone.

I chatted to Frank about this and that. The ring. The Grace. Leanne. I said should we go have a cup of tea or sit on the swings. Frank said no. Too risky. Leanne's friends might be around. We stayed at the bus stop.

Frank looked at his watch. An hour had gone by. Leanne would be wondering where they were.

"When do you get a day off again?" Frank asked me.

"Don't know. This time next week?"

"Meet us again."

He winked at me. A rush of blood to my heart. A wink was all it took. He was still on my side.

I kissed Ali goodbye. Kissed Frank too, on his shiny noggin. He flinched, tried to block. Failed. Smiled. Slapped my cheek.

"Next Sunday then?" I said.

Frank nodded. "We'll go somewhere no one'll see you."

"I can tell you more next time. About what I'm up to. Who knows, I might even be done."

"We'll have a retirement party for you," he said. "You can take Ali swimming."

"Nice one."

"Careful lad. Wherever it is you're going. I can't help you."
"Better learn to look after myself then, eh?"
"Yeah," he said. "You'd better."

Chapter Thirteen

No sign of Mossie at the shop next morning. His Honda was gone. Raz let me in and handed me the keys to the Astra.

"Where to, then?" I said.

"Litherland."

I shat myself.

Too close to my old place. God knew who I might meet. The pizza guys. The mates and rellies of the dead lad. Even Leanne sometimes popped up there. Paterson never told me what to do if that happened. It was for me to work out, he said.

We took Upper Parly then drove through town. Out again up Scottie Road and into Bootle. Up behind the Strand. I crapped myself whenever we stopped at lights. Watched people crossing, wondering if someone'd clock me. Breathed again when I turned off east, up the A-road, over a roundabout.

Litherland.

Raz made me turn left. Pocket of wealth. Trees lining the road. Big houses. He had me park by one. Big old red-brick job. Curly iron gate and bushy front garden.

"This your place?" I said.

"Ay." He grinned. "Lord o' the manor!" He chuckled and slapped me on the shoulder. Hopped out. Squeaked the gate and went up the garden path.

I stepped out my side and locked the Astra. Saw the red Honda parked across the street.

I walked after Raz through the gate. Ducked the bushes and ivy along the path to the front porch.

Mossie was there on the front doorstep. He was all dressed up for something. Long shirty dress under his cord jacket. Baggy trousers.

Raz patted him on the shoulder and slapped his cheek. Well done for something. He turned to me as I reached the porch.

"Alright Azo, la'. Me and Mossie going out."

"Eh? Where?"

"Need to know. Need you stay here. Take care the lad."

"Lad?"

"Hanzi."

"You what?"

Raz pointed inside the house.

"Sit with him," he said. "Watch telly. Make sure he don't break anything."

He'd never told me babysitting was part of the job. I didn't whinge though. Thought of Paterson. Had to try and make the most of it.

"When are you back?" I asked Raz.

No answer. They were off down the path and crossing the street to the Honda.

I stepped into the house and shut the front door behind me.

Not much to it inside. High ceilings, old wooden staircase. No varnish. No carpet. Bare plaster on the walls. Hall with doors off it. Under the stairs, a smaller cellar door, locked.

I went in the back room.

He was sat there in an old armchair with the telly on. He wasn't watching it. He was staring out the window at the trees.

Little lad. About ten, eleven. Anorak on, like he'd just got there. Bit of dried noodle down the front.

He turned and glanced at me when I walked in. Right glum look on his gob. He turned back to the window.

"Alright mate," I said.

Nothing.

I sat down on the sofa. Crappy old thing with broken springs. I sank right down into it.

"You not hot in that coat?" I said.

He looked at me with round black eyes. Blank. He looked at my feet.

I said it again, pointing at my own jacket. He looked down. Brushed off the scrap of noodle. Kept his coat on.

I looked around me. Saw a kitchen through the door. Table, sink. Kettle. Spar bag with shopping.

"You want something to eat, mate?" I said. "Cup of tea?"

I found the gizmo and turned down the telly.

"Do you speak English, lad?" I said. "English?"

He stared at me for a sec then looked back at the window.

I went in the kitchen and looked in Mossie's Spar bag. Tea, milk. Penguin bickies. I put the kettle on and washed out some mugs.

When the tea was ready I took it through to Hanzi. Put it down with a bowl of sugar lumps and a Penguin. He opened the wrapper. As he was munching it, I tiptoed out into the hall to have a look around.

The house was almost empty. Yellow Pages in the hall. Menu for pizzas. Same place I used to work for.

I walked upstairs. Four bedrooms on the first floor. Attic up top. Little Reebok rucksack in one of the bedrooms that must have been Hanzi's. Pants and socks.

A noise down in the hall. Rattling.

I legged it down the staircase, thumping and creaking on the bare boards. Got down there as the front door slammed behind him.

I caught up with him as he was fiddling with the gate. Put my hand on his shoulder.

"Come off it, lad," I said. "You can't... "

BANG. He lamped me on the gob with his little fist. Then again, in the bollocks.

I crumpled to my knees. Didn't stay down for long though. I tucked the pain away deep inside like Ralph taught me. Sprang back up. Got my arms round the lad's ribs and tried to drag him sideways up the path. He pounded me on the head. Caught me on the eardrum. I went deaf for a sec. Dizzy. Faint. I didn't let go of him.

He lunged up and bit my ear.

I drew my breath in and tried not to roar. He slipped out of my grasp. I felt blood down my neck. He legged back to the gate and I was after him again. Arms round him. He elbowed me. Raked his heel down my shins. He'd almost wriggled free. His hands yanked at the gate.

A curtain twitched across the road.

I snapped. I legged him up and he hit the ground, behind the hedge where no one could see him. He went quiet and wheezed when my foot hit his stomach.

I pulled him up on the porch steps by the hair. Slung him through the front door. Down the hall. Into the lounge. Shoved him onto the settee.

There was a key in that sitting room door. And another in the one to the kitchen beyond it. I turned the sound up on the telly and locked him in.

I leaned my back against the door in the hall. Sank to the floor, shuddering.

This voice there was, inside me. Some kind of judge. It knew I should have gone down for killing the lad in The Grace. Now it was watching everything I did. Well Azo, lad, it said. You done a lot of bad things, but at least you always knew the reason. Till now. How's this for a new job, eh. Beating up children.

My breath steadied after a few minutes. But I'd not forgive myself. I'd played this game to get myself out of trouble. I should have known it would just mean more dirty fighting.

Two hours later I heard the front door open. I was sitting in the back room on the sofa. Split lip. Bleeding ear. Hanzi in the armchair next to me. Graze on his head from the garden gravel. Calmed down, he had. Scared of me now. All white. He went whiter when he saw Raz come in cracking his knuckles.

"How did you get on, la'?" Raz said. He frowned. Looked at the lad. Put on this big stern voice. "Hanzi? You been a good lad?"

The kid got up and ran past Raz, trembling. He legged it upstairs to his room. Raz let him go.

I stood up. Shifted my feet to ease my aching bollocks. "He tried to do one," I said to Raz. "I grabbed him. He went mad."

Raz clapped me on the shoulder and winked. "I reckoned you'd be up to the job."

He knew what would happen, the big shady twat. It was a test.

"Don't worry," he said. "I'll not call the filth!"

I thought of Paterson. How I'd tell him all this and stitch Raz up. Made me feel a bit better. Only a bit.

The front door opened again and shut. Mossie came in.

Another young lad with him.

About fifteen. Hard bristles on his chin. Big dirty parka jacket, trackie bottoms and old white trainies, stained grey with skank. He nodded at me and Raz showed him upstairs. Put him in the same room as Hanzi.

I looked in on them before I headed back to the shop. The new lad was sitting on one of the beds next to Hanzi, chatting away to him. Talked like a Manc. He was speaking in English but somehow he seemed to be making Hanzi understand. The little lad was smiling for a change.

I stood and watched them for a sec. They looked up and saw me. The Manc nodded at me again. Hanzi glared.

Raz said he'd sleep the night there. I had to get the train back to Tocky. I ran into Mossie coming up the garden path. He saw the shock on my face.

"Hanzi acting up?" he said.

I lit a Regal.

"Don't worry about the little lad, mate," Mossie said. "He'll be alright now. You should have seen the last one who tried to get away."

I didn't want to know. I was feeling sick enough in my belly already. But it was worth hearing, for Paterson's sake. I made myself ask.

"What happened?"

He smirked. "Raz took him in the cellar."

"Where is he now?"

"He went to do his duty. Like we all must. No running and no grassing. Raz doesn't like it."

"Better not cross him then, eh?"

"Better not."

I called Paterson later from my flat. Calm as I could. But I broke down when I told him about Hanzi.

Paterson said he knew how I felt. Sometimes we had to do bad things to do good.

"You're a right saint, you," I said.

"And you are one of my best assets."

"You said I could see my lad if I did well." I didn't let on I'd seen him already. I was fishing around for Paterson's blessing. Least he could do, eh. I'd held up my side. "So?" I said. "When?"

"When I say you can."

Chapter Fourteen

I was on shop duty on my own the next few days. Working the till and shuffling chocky bars around. All quiet. On the Friday morning Raz showed up. He told me two more lads had moved into his house.

He handed me the car keys. We shut the shop and headed off.

He made me drive south and turn first left.

"We not heading to Litherland?" I asked him.

"Ay, la'. Little pit-stop first though."

"What for?"

"Pack yourself a bag."

We'd reached my building.

I parked the Astra and tugged the handbrake up.

"We going somewhere?"

"Oh ay, la'," he said.

"How long will I be gone then? Need to know how many pairs of boxies to take, eh?"

He laughed and thumped my shoulder.

"Call it a work trip, la'. Business class!"

I bobbed up to my flat and stuffed some clothes in a rucksack.

I felt sick driving over to Litherland. Kept thinking I'd see someone I knew. No way round it, though. If I got spotted, I'd have to work something out.

I rolled the Astra into the crescent and stopped by Raz's front gate.

A right scout camp it was now. Hanzi was hoovering in the hall when I came in. The Manc was washing up dishes in the kitchen. The lino was wet from mopping and the whole place smelt of bleach. The windows were open airing out all the rooms. Mossie was sat in an armchair in the back.

Raz stomped around checking on it all, like some big hairy Mother Hubbard on crack. He pointed through the kitchen window to the back garden. Two others there, hanging up sheets on a line. Pair of skinny black lads in matching turquoise trackies.

There were sleeping bags laid out on all the beds. Raz had moved into the downstairs room at the front. Another one across the hall from it, not taken yet. He led us upstairs. Hanzi and the Manc were sharing one room with the two other lads next door. That left one other room untaken on the other side, looking out on the back garden.

On the landing Raz pointed to the ceiling. Ladder going up through a trap door. Attic. He made me climb it.

Another bedroom up there. Sloping ceiling, skylight and a folding camp bed.

Raz looked at me.

"Get lost," I said.

"Ay, la'. Good for you this way. Save you rent. Food. Stick with all the others in the house of lads. Make friends. Brothers."

I stared at the camp bed, then out through the skylight at the high tree branches in the back garden. Green leaves and grey slate roofs beyond.

This was what Paterson was after. Have me right on the inside.

"Big step for you," Raz said. "Move you up the ladder." He grinned and slapped me on the shoulder. "Better like this. You help me out here. We help you. Deal."

Time for my grateful orphan act.

"Raz, mate," I said. "Are you sure?"

Tears in my voice. It must have been a real Oscar job, because Raz put his arm round me. Hot sweat from his armpit soaked onto me through his t-shirt.

"Look Azo lad," he said. "Truth is, I need your help. These lads got nothing. Like you said you didn't, when I met you. Well now they got me. Me and Mossie feed them. Roof over them. Need someone to help though. Mentor, like. Someone more their age."

I might have believed that Good Samaritan bollocks if he'd not set me up like that with Hanzi.

"What you running here, Raz?" I asked him. "Shelter?"

"More than that, la'. These lads are here to learn. School of life!"

He squeezed me deeper in his pit.

"That's where you come in, la'. Teach them stuff."

"Like what?"

"Like what I saw you giving that lad in the shop. That neck-lock. Class. You told me about your boxing an' all. What you learned at that ring. You useful to us, lad. Gifted. Trained."

He was whispering in my ear.

"Me and Mossie teach them lads there's something to fight for," he said. "You teach them how to fight." He pinched my cheek. "We teach them to live. You teach them to stay alive."

I smiled. Tried to look keen. Hoped he'd let me out of his armpit.

"Why though, Raz?" I said. "Why you helping these lads?"

"'Cos I can."

"But who's paying? Who were you off to see the other day?"

He closed his eyes and shushed me, laying a finger on my lips.

"Mossie teach the good book. The bits that suit him. He talk to the people with the money. You and me, we're the ones who get stuff done."

"What stuff?"

"You'll see. I'll teach you things that'll make you angry. Make you fight. Make you change the world."

"Can I still have my Sundays off?"

He chuckled and nodded.

"You going to do great things, la'," he said. "You and me together. I'm the Big Daddy here. You the Big Brother!"

"Thanks, Raz, mate," I said. "For the room. For everything. I'll not forget it."

Raz hugged me closer. The doorbell rang downstairs.

"Here he is. The new lad."

This one'd got there on his own. I caught a glimpse of him in the hall as Mossie opened the door. Black tracksuit with white three-stripes. Mossie took him upstairs.

Raz rounded up the others and had them line up in the back

garden.

"This is Azo, lads," he said. "Anyone starts on you, he sort them out. You need anything, you worried or got troubles, you can talk to him."

I worked along the line, shaking hands with them like we were about to play footie.

First up was little Hanzi. His thick black hair and eyebrows. His sad eyes.

"Sorry I hit you, mate," I said. "Hit me back if you want. I won't do nothing."

He held his hand limp round mine and looked at me. Smiled for a sec, but not with his eyes. They stared right through me. Wait till I'm bigger, the eyes said. Then I'll hit you back.

Next to him was the Manc in his skanky old parka. Lee, his name was. He'd made friends with Hanzi.

Then the two in turquoise trackies. Twins. About fifteen, sixteen. Tall and lanky with short curly hair.

They told me their names.

"Casho," said the first one.

"Ayax," said the other.

Their voices had hardly broken, but their handshakes were deadly. They were more edgy than the others. Gangly, hungry-looking, like a pair of wolves. Matching grazes on their knuckles.

When I thought all the handshaking was done, Mossie came out with the new one.

Lean Asian lad. Handsome. Older than the others. Eighteen? Nineteen? Bumfluff moustache and fresh face. Stocky though. These thick upper arms. Chunky thighs. Massive bulge in his trackie pants. He came straight up to me and shook my hand. He held himself up straight, shoulders back. Stared right in my eye.

He looked well up himself. I didn't trust him.

"Azo. Rodney," he said. "How are you doing."

West Indian twang.

We shook hands hard, testing each other's grip. He pulled me off balance. I steadied myself and tugged him towards me. It was his turn to steady his feet.

He smiled as we let go.

Something about him put me on guard. Something not right. Too cocky he was. Too happy.

The others were still standing in line. Rodney turned and went to shake hands with each of them. Like he was older and smarter. He joked with Casho and Ayax. Patted Hanzi on the head and ruffled his hair.

I felt Raz's hand on my shoulder.

"One more to come," he said. "Then we're a full house."

He pulled a load of tenners from his shorts and handed them to me. Then he dug in the other pocket and found a bit of crumpled paper. List of groceries scrawled on it.

"Need you to drive to Tesco's, la'."

I went off in the Astra and did a big shop for us all. Crisps, oven chips, ice cream. On the way back, I pulled over in a side street, killed the engine and slipped out the Nokia.

I was checked into Raz's House of Lads. I called Paterson and told him all about it.

Chapter Fifteen

The weather broke that night. Next morning the sky was grey and spitting. Raz had us all put our coats on and walk with him down to the docks.

A right sight we were. Six lads and this big scally leading us along. A pig car went by. This rozzer stared out at us. They didn't stop though. Better things to do. Or maybe he spotted me and knew the deal. Had Paterson told all the bizzies about me? Anyway. They weren't my arse-ache any more. It was the locals I was worried about.

We fetched up on this high patch of waste ground. Green weeds gleaming in the drizzle. A street of old warehouses below with rubbish in the gutter. Old pub on the corner, boarded up. Scrap yard. Then the docks. Those massive blue cranes and stacks of shipping crates. Red, blue, green. Rusty. Some with Chinese writing on. Some with Arabic. At the seafront, white metal windmills turning in the mist.

Raz gazed over at it all.

"The New York of Europe," he said. He stared round at us. "That's what they called Liverpool. The warehouse of the empire. Not anymore."

We shuffled our feet and shivered. The rain was coming down harder.

"It's just a few crappy crates nowadays," he said. "But back then, more freight passed through this port than you can dream of. Tobacco. Cotton. And don't forget the sugar!"

He did this spoddy chinny-reckon face and put on this daft posh voice. "Tell me, lahds, how does one caht down tannes of sugar cane in the Caribbee-arn to ship it over to Liverpewl? Does one get up off one's rich fat arse and caht it oneself?"

The lads looked at each other. Rodney spoke.

"Slaves," he said.

Raz nodded. He let the word hang there. "Right, lad," he said. "That's how Liverpool was built."

65

He led us to the far side of the waste ground. Someone had dumped a chunk of giant conky piping there. Huge grey thing, nearly big enough to stand up in. Raz stepped in and bashed around in it, kicking out old cans and bottles.

I watched him. He looked like some old meff settling down to sleep in the park. The mad bastard. Is that all there was to him? Some crap about what happened hundreds of years ago?

He stooped in the mouth of the pipe and faced us.

"They stopped bringing the slaves through them docks," he said. "After a while. But there's other stuff coming from Africa now."

"What stuff, Raz?" I said.

"Naughty stuff. In them containers. Too many to search them all. Used to be dockers who'd handle the cargo. Keep an eye. Fired most of them, didn't they. Now they going to reap the storm."

He sat us all down inside the pipe and made each of the lads tell his story.

Casho and Ayax went first. They took turns to talk. Patchy English they had. But we all understood.

They ran away when some clan killed their mum and dad, Casho said. Fourteen, they were. But they had their heads screwed on. Robbed enough money to get out of Somalia. Boats and the backs of trucks. All the way to Liverpool. They had cousins who'd been there for years. The cousins didn't want to know them though. Things were mixed up back where they came from. They met Mossie at the Mosque.

The two lads stopped talking. Raz sat there nodding and let it sink in.

"Tell us more about your mum and dad," he said. "What happened?"

Ayax couldn't bear it. He clutched his brother's arm and tried to bury his face behind him while Casho told us about the day the clansmen came to their village.

He tried to talk us through it all. The wars and the leaders. The past. I was lost, but Raz sat there nodding, like he knew it all already. When it looked like Casho was going to cry too,

Raz growled and made him go on. About their mother. Ayax curled into a ball.

Casho finished talking and pulled his brother into his arms. None of us spoke. Raz got up, stooping in the low tunnel, and stepped towards them. He gently lifted Casho's hands, put his own arms round Ayax and hoisted him up standing. He wiped the tears off Ayax's face with two big thumbs and hugged him to his chest.

"Alright, lad," he said. "We all here with you now."

Ayax tightened his arms around Raz's back and mumbled through the tears.

"Thank you."

Next to their story, Manc Lee's sounded like *In The Night Garden*. He reckoned he had all this behavioural crap that messed with his head. That and a sheet or two of speed, eh. It wasn't really why his mum and stepdad chucked him out. That was after he started going to the wrong kind of meetings in a room above a chippy. They were run by Mossie's mates.

He still had a crooked finger from where his stepdad slammed the door.

"I'm a lippy twat," he said. "Been chinned enough times, you'd think I'd shut up and sit down. I don't."

I liked him. He'd learned some crap off Mossie and his mates, but he didn't shove it down your throat. He still knew how to have a laugh.

Raz coughed and shifted on his feet where he was squatting down in the mouth of the tube. "Tell 'em the best bit, Lee lad," he said.

The Manc widened his eyes, all harmless like he didn't know what Raz meant. It was a crap act. Raz frowned and the Manc went on. He'd spent two years living in a squat in Moss Side. He learned how to take care of himself for real.

"He learned to pick locks," said Raz, beaming.

Mossie had found him giving out leaflets by a book shop in Saint Helens.

Raz dipped into the pockets of his Berghaus, pulled out two bags of Nik-Naks and handed them round to us. We sat munching the powdery crisps while Rodney started talking.

Paterson had said he wanted me to tell him how people talked. His spods trained me for what to look for. How to break people's voices down. Rodney's was all over the place. Caribbean, Indian, northern. It did my head in. I needed to suss him out. I couldn't.

His mum and dad came over from Trinidad in the seventies, settled in Toxteth and had Rodney there. He reckoned his dad got his head kicked in by the bizzies in the riots and was never the same since. He was right enough to jizz you out though, wasn't he, I wanted to say. Toxteth riots, my arse. Meant to be eighteen, this lad. His dad would have been wrong in the head for years before he had Rodney. He chucked Toxteth in there because he knew it was the kind of thing Raz wanted to hear.

"Hey, Raz," I said, butting into Rodney's story. "Was you around in Tocky in eighty-one? Did you see it all go off?"

Raz stuck a long knobbly Nik-Nak in his gob and talked as he crunched it.

"Nah," he says. "Eighty-one I weren't in the 'Pool. I were somewhere else."

That look in his eye. Same one I saw the first day I met him. Like he was remembering something nasty.

He didn't care how likely Rodney's story sounded. He could do the maths. But he knew what he liked. What mattered was Rodney thought it was true.

Rodney's dad ended up in some loonie bin and his mum headed back to Trinidad. Rodney ran away. Streets. Squats. One night in a Syrian cafe he tried to sell a rose to a man called Mossie.

Rodney stood up and stepped out of the concrete tube. Paced around and stretched. Looked up at the sky and stuck his tongue out to taste the rain. It had eased off. He stepped back in the tube.

So that was his story. I looked round at the lads. They were all staring at him. None of them smiling. None of them thinking what a scrote. Great. They'd all swallowed it.

"Where were you?"

Raz looked round. It was Ayax. He wiped his nose and asked again.

"In eighty-one," he said. "You said not in Liverpool. Where?"

Raz screwed up his bag of Nik Naks and licked bits out of his teeth. He frowned. Then his gob split into a grin.

"I were in a war."

Ayax nodded.

"I didn't go to fight," Raz said. "I were a doctor."

Manc Lee tittered.

"Yeah," Raz said. "I were a smartarse. Been to uni. Thought that could help win wars. Soon learned better. I ended up fighting like all the rest."

"Where?" Ayax said.

"Afghanistan."

I felt my skin tingle.

Ayax nodded. The Manc rustled his crisp packet. Then all was still.

"Helping us out, this country was," Raz said. "Helping the Muj fight the Ruskies. Food and drugs to heal their children. Them friendly Yanks and Britskies. That's why they sent Raz there. Young doctor man. Helpy helpy. Silly silly. Gets slotted by a Rusky shell."

He pointed at his lazy eye. His left one by the scar. He tapped it with a finger nail. Glass.

"In the hills," he said. "In a cave. Looked after by the Muj. Liked it there, I did. Liked the folks. Most of all I liked the poppy. Liked it all so much I stayed fifteen years. Learned the lingo. Stopped talking like a uni spod."

He picked a scrap of Nik-Nak from his teeth.

"As long as it suited them Brit and Yank pigdogs, they helped us," he went on. "Sent us guns to slot them Ruskies with. Twenty years on, they change their minds. Didn't like the Muj no more. Bombing them. Us. We still had the weapons they give us. But not the food or meds!"

Raz twisted his neck and flobbed a big greeny out into the rain.

"It did us proud, this country," he went on. "Just like it did with the sugar. Grew fat on slavery, it did. Filled this city with red-brick mansions. Azo. Did you grow up in one of them?"

"I grew up in shite."

"So all that empire. All them riches. Still left us living in that."

I looked round at the lads. They were lapping it up. Their eyes locked on Raz. I tried to lock all his crap in my head for Paterson.

"It's done you proud, hasn't it, this country?" Raz said. "You ready to show you're grateful?"

He pointed at Hanzi, sitting next to the Manc with his knees under his chin.

"How about this lad here," Raz said. "How many chances you think he's had in life? Well, I tell you."

He sniffed and curled his lip.

"He been used. Begging. Handing the money to his boss every night. Till along comes Uncle Raz and sets him free."

He moved over and sat down next to Hanzi. Patted him on the shoulder.

"Well today, Hanzi's going to be the boss," Raz said. "First time in his life now. Hanzi."

He stood up. Stooped and stepped out of the pipe. We followed him. Hanzi first.

Raz strode to the low fence of the playground and stood looking out at the docks. He put his hand round Hanzi's shoulder again.

"Down there." Raz pointed. "See it? That big metal box?"

Hanzi nodded.

"That's where your old boss lives," Raz said. "He owes me money."

An empty street down the rise, between the waste ground and the docks. Old shipping container next to the kerb among the scraps of old carpet and chip papers. One end of it pried half open.

The drizzle had stopped. The air was still and close. The crackly sound of a radio coming from inside the container.

"You go in there, lad," Raz said. "You get me money. Money?"

He made that greedy rubby sign with his thumb and middle finger. Hanzi understood. Someone had taught him that before.

He nodded three times, quickly. Like he might get hit if he didn't do a good job.

"You get his money," Raz went on. He knelt down beside Hanzi with his hand on his shoulder, his face close to the boy's. "Then you show him how grateful you are."

Hanzi was nodding like mad now. His eyes wide. Raz reached in an inside pocket of his Berghaus. Took out this little black tube. Flicked his wrist.

A steel cosh, a foot and a half long. It sprung out of the handle and narrowed to a little black knob at the end.

I looked over my shoulder for that bizzie car. Nothing. I looked back at Hanzi. He had the cosh in his hand now.

I felt sick.

Hanzi looked up at Raz. Raz nodded. His top lip unpeeled, up over his sticky-out tooth. Smiling.

Hanzi ran off down the slope, the cosh in his hand, wagging as he went like a magic wand. He rounded the crate and went up to the half-open door at the near end. Pried it wider open with a groan and creak of metal.

We watched him step up and vanish inside.

Chapter Sixteen

For ten seconds all was quiet. Just the crackle of the radio.

The sun had pricked through one of the clouds. I was sweating under my anorak. I held my breath. The other lads too. Our eyes on the door of the crate.

Then the noise.

Banging. Shrieking. Moaning.

I made to run down the slope but Raz reached out and grabbed my collar. Dragged me back to stand beside him. I tried to hold still and stop trembling.

All hush again. For ages.

And then there was Hanzi, running back up the slope. Panting. The cosh still in his hand and something blue in the other.

He stopped in front of Raz, holding the cosh down by his side. Blood and black hairs on it.

Hanzi looked up at Raz. At me. A flash of something awful in his eyes. Some animal thing that tore right through me.

He held out the blue thing. Little steel safe box. Raz took it and patted him on the head.

I touched Hanzi on the arm and tried to gently take the cosh from his right hand. His little black eyes darted at me. Again, that tiger-flash in them. His hand tightened on the weapon. I squeezed his shoulder and talked to him, all calming like.

"Good lad," I said. "Alright."

He let go.

Raz put his arm round the boy's shoulders. "Mr Hanzi, ladies and gents," he said.

The lads had stayed quiet till then, watching. Now they blew up. Whooped. Cheered. Crowded round Hanzi, slapping him on the back and messing his hair.

I wiped the cosh on the grass and close it back up in its handle. I was about to slip it in the pocket of my coat when Raz called and reached out for it. He took it from me, turned and handed it to Ayax. The lad grabbed it. Snapped his wrist, locking the weapon out again in one go.

His turn.

"All together now, lads," Raz said. His eyes went wide and mad, his lips snarled back. "Get down there, the lot of yous. Take that shack to fucking pieces."

The five lads roared and slithered down the slope.

I looked at Raz. He winked. "Not you, la'," he said. "Best I keep you on the bench. Head coach!"

I looked back down at the container. The lads piling in through the opening. Banging noises from inside. Rodney got there last, strutted along the length of it and slipped behind.

Raz put a meaty hand round the back of my neck and shook me. Matey. Like we were all in it together.

Rodney showed up again, round the far end of the crate. He'd found an iron bar from somewhere. He jumped up on the roof of the shipping box and started putting dents in it, trying to bust through the rusty metal.

Raz cheered them on. Then he couldn't help joining in. He let go of my neck and bent down. Picked up a brick and lashed it down the slope. It clanged and bounced off the box.

I cacked myself all the way home trying to calm the lads down. Looking over my shoulder for that pig car while they ran along hooting and yelling.

Raz left me to it and plodded ahead on his own. Nice one. That was my job then, eh. Keep the lads in line once he'd stirred them up. I had to keep yelling to hush them till we were back at the house.

Soon as we were home Raz got a big pan of macaroni cheese on the go. I sorted the lads out. Made them go up to their rooms and change out of their wet stuff. Not Manc Lee though. He had bits of broken mirror stuck in his knuckles.

I'd calmed down myself now we were back inside. My hands had stopped shaking. I sat on the sofa with Lee and picked out the shards. Swabbed his hand and bandaged it up. All stuff they taught me inside, on Paterson's orders. Raz saw. Asked me where I learned first aid. I told him my mum was a nurse. It was true.

Raz sent Casho and Ayax out in the back yard with the money box and some tools. I heard them bashing around getting it open. Soon enough they came back in. Five hundred quid's worth of tenners in their hands. They handed it over to Raz. Anxy look on their faces. Raz counted it. Eyeballed them. He knew they'd not nicked any. They were too shit-scared of him to do that.

"The spoils," he said. "Of this war they make us fight."

He stashed the dosh in his room. He locked it and went in the kitchen. We all followed him in and sat down for lunch together like some big nasty family, pouring each other squash and passing the Daddies' Sauce.

"You done well today, lads," he told them. "Listened to old Raz. Told us your stories. Spoke truth without fear. Fought bravely for them spoils. But hear the rule. No more stealing unless I say. No scrapping unless it's with Azo on them mats. No mischief. Or you bring the pigs down on us. And you'll answer to me."

After lunch it was still pissing with rain so we stayed in. Raz sat the lads all down in the back room to talk at them. He let me off though.

"Take a break, la'," he said. "You done good looking after the lads today. You're management now!"

He shut himself in the sitting room with his little class. His voice drifted through the door, growing louder as he got well into it. I put my ear to the wood and listened in for a bit. More of the crap he talked down at the docks. He was on about Syria now.

I went out the front door, down the garden path and walked round the corner to a playground. Sat on a bench and got the phone out of my pocket.

He wanted to know everything. About the house, the street. The lads. Names and what they looked like and where they were from.

I told him about the talk Raz had given us down by the docks. The lads' stories. Raz's. How they'd all been headhunted by Mossie.

Paterson didn't sound shocked by any of it. He said "Hmm" a lot. This tightness in his voice that I'd not heard before. I wondered if he was stressed. Wondered something else too. Deep down. I wondered if he'd spied on me. If he knew I'd been to see Ali.

I told him what Raz had said about the container ships.

"He's smuggling something through the docks?" Paterson said.

"He said there's too many of those containers to check every one."

"He's right."

I told him about the feller they battered with the cosh. "He's using these lads," I said when I was done.

"Hmm."

"He knows they've got nothing. He can make them do whatever he says."

"That's the kind of evil we're trying to fight all over the world, Azo. Those lads are lucky you're here, doing your bit."

"So will all this be enough to put Raz away?"

"Why, Azo? Have you got it all worked out?"

"Won't you need me to point the finger at him?"

"No thanks, lad. Last thing we need's a murderer standing up for us in court. You keep your head down and carry on digging."

I stood up off the park bench and paced around the swings.

"We've chaps all over the place working through your leads," he said. "You just keep the calls coming. Names, places. Times. Keep an eye out for guns. Watch, listen, tell. Don't worry about trying to nail anyone. Your stuff is safe with me. Some of it I'll pass along, but if you've a big nugget that could get traced back to you, I'll sit on it to keep you safe."

"Can I see my kid?"

I asked him every time. I'd already done it without his blessing, hadn't I. But it didn't feel too safe running around behind his back.

"Sure," he said. "If you do your job."

I made myself sound calm. Mustn't look like I was losing it.

"They got me living in Litherland now," I said. "Stone's throw from my old place. What if I see someone I know?"

I heard him sniff as he took that in. He paused. I chewed my nail. Then he spoke.

"Azo. Are you threatening to mess this up unless you can see your boy?"

"I'm just saying. What if someone spots me? Someone who knows what happened in The Grace? If Raz finds out I killed a lad he'll wonder why I'm not inside. He'll sniff around. He'll add it up. And it most likely won't even be him who slots me. He'll set the lads on me. They'll cosh me to death."

Paterson sighed. "If you have any bother round there, call me."

"And what'll you do?"

"I'll make the bother go away."

I couldn't help pushing it.

"Look, I've done all you said. I've kept my mouth shut. Will you not let me see my kid just once?"

He sighed again. Like all the weight of the world was on his shoulders.

"I can give you more money. How about that? You can spend it, or save it up for Ali later."

I said nothing for a bit. He'd been leaving me envelopes of cash. It had kept me from starving before I moved into the house. But not much more.

"Well?" he said.

"Go on then."

"Good man. If you do well, you'll see him soon enough," he said. "Keep the calls coming."

"That's all you really care about isn't it? You're like Raz. You're using me."

"We talked about this, Azo. What you do for me can save lives."

"So to stop Raz using them lads, you use lads like me. Where does it all end?"

"Stay put in that house and you may find out."

Sod that, I thought. The next day was Sunday.

Chapter Seventeen

I got back from seeing Ali at six in the evening. As I reached the front gate, Mossie was pulling away in his Honda.

"Where's he off?" I asked Raz as I stepped through the front door.

"Going to pick up the new kid," he said.

The lads had been having a rest. They came down from their rooms as I was setting the table.

Raz got chips in. Treat for Sunday night. We sat round the kitchen table, all seven of us. Greasy papers strewn all over. Raz at the head, joking and laughing. He poured coke in our glasses and spooned out ice cream for afters.

When the washing-up was done, he sent me out to the garden.

Another of those weird wet summer days it had been, but the sky was clear now. The tufty grass was dry and yellow but the rain had soggied it up.

I went to the wooden shed at the bottom of the lawn.

All this sport stuff inside. Crazy-golf clubs. Flyaway footies. Gym mats stacked on top of each other. And what Raz sent me for: a cricket set.

He took us down the park.

I'd never touched a bat and ball in my life, but Raz knew what he was doing. He hopped around in his trainies and his green cap, showing Casho, Ayax and Hanzi how to bowl. Pivot the shoulders, swing the arms. Bicep brushing the ear. And with the bat. Knees bent, arse out like you wanted to get bummed.

Casho and Ayax picked it up quick. They started tonking it all over the park. Raz ran around fielding, catching and stumping and cackling. Rodney was good too. He helped Raz coach me and the lads. Patted them on the shoulder all the time, like he was in charge. Got right on my wick.

It was a boss laugh though. When we got Ayax out at last,

77

the Manc stepped in to bat. Then Hanzi. He didn't last long. Then Rodney bowled Casho. By the end it was me and Rodney. Him hitting the big shots and calling the runs. He looked like he'd stay in forever. He whacked one towards Hanzi, thinking the lad would spoon it up and he'd get an easy two. Then out of nowhere came Raz. Yelled at Hanzi to throw it to him halfway. Fielded it, flicked his wrist and cracked it onto Rodney's wicket from twenty yards.

He jogged over to give high fives to Hanzi. The little lad smiled.

I sat on my heels and watched Raz romping around like a big kid. He paused for breath, leaning over with his hands on his knees, and looked at his watch.

"Nearly ten." He yelled at the lads to pack up the kit. "Home," he said. "Meet the new kid."

Rodney whacked the ball off again in a huff. It whizzed over the far side of the park. Raz walked over to have a word with him. Called to me as he went. Told me to jog and get it.

It had landed in a flower bed across the far path.

I stepped in the squishy soil, leaned over and picked the ball out. Hopped back onto the path and lobbed it towards the lads. Rodney trotted forward and fielded it.

I was about to jog back when I heard a voice behind me. Rough, dopey. Blocked nose.

"Uv yer gorra spurr ciggie thurr mayce?"

I looked at him. Skanky-looking twat. Sick pale skin, sticky-out ears. Baggy sunken eyes.

"Sorry, mate," I muttered.

I started walking away. Glanced at him again, over my shoulder. I stopped.

Greasy hair. Scraggy neck covered in spots.

I crapped myself.

He was wearing the same manky tracksuit as before. The second lad I decked in The Grace. The dead one's mate. He still had the scar on his top lip from where I'd hit him.

"Sorry mate," I muttered again.

He was looking right at me. I turned my face away and carried on walking. But the voice came again, weak and raw.

"'Ey, laz."

I stopped walking. Stayed calm. Turned around.

He stared hard at me. Looked mad. Then scared. His face crumpled. He coughed and spat, turned and stumbled away.

I went after him. He walked faster.

"Come 'ead mate," I said. "Let me talk to you."

He started running, yelling back at me down the path. "I call the bizzies. They should have sent you down."

I broke into a run myself.

"I get Gary's folks on you," he yelled.

I tried to stay calm.

"I just want to talk to you," I shouted. I didn't know what about though. What I really wanted to do was call Paterson. I fumbled my phone out of my pocket and looked at the time. Almost five to ten. I'd be late back. Raz would be mad.

The lad turned to face me. Got his balls up now he was a way off. He pointed a finger.

"Keep looking over your shoulder," he yelled. "We'll stab the lot of yous. You first of all, nig-nog. You're fuckin' dead!"

He darted to the right through one of the park gates.

I squinted through the trees. The lads were gathering up their stuff. Raz was standing there, looking around. Wondering where I'd got to. I didn't know what story I'd tell him. No time to think though. I turned my back on them, ran to the gate and out of the park.

The lad was heading down a side road.

I followed him, creeping behind trees and cars. People stared, wondering what I was up to. On her majesty's secret knobcheese, I wanted to tell them. Go home. Nothing to see.

The lad slowed down. He thought he'd lost me but I kept him in sight. He turned off west. Then right, onto a main road towards the docks.

Left again. This web of old terraces. At the bottom of one there was a battered wire fence with a gap in it. Then a slope down to the railway.

I caught up with him on the other side of the gap. Legged him up as he was crouching to slide down the embankment.

He rolled to the bottom, swearing and grunting.

I slithered down after him on my arse in the soil. Wet and oily it was. Scattered with cans and needles. I grabbed him as he rolled in a heap at the bottom. Hoisted him up by his trackie top and sat him on his arse on the slope.

He tried to spring up and leg it. I slammed him down again.

"I just want to talk to you."

"Fuck off, I said."

I looked up the slope to the street. Head lights sweeping over as the cars swished by. Shadows of people walking past.

He started yelling. I smacked him in the gob. He stopped. Looked at me. Scared now.

"Where you off to, lad?" I asked him.

He said nothing.

"Do your mate's folks live round here?"

His look gave it away. Over my shoulder, towards the slate-roofs across the track. Back yards. Pants hanging on lines.

"Listen lad," I said. "I'm sorry about what happened. I'll make it up to you."

I took out my phone and dialled Paterson's number. I could have him send someone to take the lad in. Stop him blowing my cover. Paterson would understand. He said he'd always be there. Said he'd make the bother go away.

It was ringing.

The lad tried to get up and bolt again. I grabbed him by the trackie top and shoved him back down. He punched me in the knackers. I half crumpled over. Dropped the phone. Dreno softened the pain though. Sharpened me up. I still had hold of him, his trackie bunched in my fist. He was trying to stand up on the slope.

I leaned forward, clicked my neck and nutted him with the side of my head. Caught him on the eye. He fell on his hip with a whimper.

I picked the phone back up out of the dirt. I held the lad still there, my fist clutching his top, my knuckles up at his collar bone digging in his throat.

The call had cut off when I dropped it. I dialled Paterson again.

He didn't answer.

The lad was looking at me. Rubbing his hip and his forehead. It was nearly dark. His eyes shone in the half-light. Scared. Hateful.

I called Paterson again. Ten rings. Twenty. No voicemail. Nothing.

I put the phone back in my pocket. Gazed across the tracks at the sun going down beyond the docks. Lighting up the cranes, slate roofs, breezeblock towers. Orange, pink, purple.

I stared at the colours and let it sink in.

No Paterson.

I was on my own. No one there for me but Raz, back at the house. Some new scrote coming in for me to bully. I saw it in my mind. Raz, looking at his watch. Badmouthing me. Wondering where I was.

The lad had another go, tearing free of my hand. His trackie ripped. He scrambled away and legged it along the embankment, heading for a spot where he could cross the tracks.

I ran after him. He fumbled something out of his pocket as he ran and put it to his ear. I closed on him. Reached out and got an arm round his scrawny neck. It felt like it'd break.

I grabbed his arm and twisted his wrist round with my free hand till he dropped it. Shiny and white. I picked it out of the mud. A slinky little smartphone. Poor little scrote. It must have cost him months' worth of dole.

He'd put a call through as he was running. Someone answered just as I got my finger on the touch-screen. I squeezed the side button, shut the phone down and slipped it in my pocket with my free hand.

I squeezed his windpipe and dragged his head down level with my waist. He started gurgling and sobbing.

"Kick my head in then, you knob," he said. "You're still dead."

I locked his neck tighter. Tried to make him shut up so I could think. He wouldn't.

"I'll tell Gary's dad," he said. His voice was strangled and thin, but somehow it came out. "He'll come after you. Even if the bizzies won't."

I looked up the slope towards the street where the headlights came and went. I dropped to my knees, wrestling the lad down with me. I tried Paterson a third time.

I counted thirty rings, then lost it. Roared. Sobbed. Sweared. Then I made myself hold it in. Swallowed it and choked it down.

The lad was too shit-up to move now.

I looked up at the sunset again. Tried to breathe. Faced this new world I was in. More alone than ever. Something settled down in me. Something nasty. I let it settle.

I saw the car lights coming and going up on Stanley Road.

I breathed slower. Calmer. I knew what I was doing. Easy, in a way. Having no choice.

It took a couple of minutes. I got both hands on his neck. Pressed on them juicy pipes either side of his windpipe. Tightened till he stopped struggling.

I heard the tracks snapping and shuddering as a train headed our way.

I held him there a minute longer then left his body on the track.

Chapter Eighteen

Numb. Blind. Trembling. I couldn't think about what I'd done, so I thought of the next worst thing: what was waiting for me when I got to the house.

Raz, wondering where I'd been. Why I'd not come back to meet the new lad. Why I wasn't there to settle them all down at bedtime.

That lying bastard Paterson. *I'll always be there, lad. I'll always answer.*

I'll teach him, I thought. I'd wreck this whole game. He could send me down if he liked. At least I'd have ended it my own way. Reckoned he was untouchable, he did. But I knew what would get to him. I'd take away the one thing he was after.

I'd do Raz.

He had it coming. More than the scrote lying on the tracks did. Raz, rounding up lads who were too poor and messed up to say no. Using them. Him and Paterson would get on great together.

Giving up? Yeah, I guess I was. I'd not last long anyway once they found that lad dead.

Ali was better off without me. I saw that now. There was a reason he lived with her and not with me. True what that lawyer had said. Not fit to, I wasn't. Who wanted a killer for a dad?

I must have stopped at the garage on the way because when I got near the house I had a pack of Regals in my hand and was smoking one. I flicked it away as I turned in the front gate.

Raz was on his way out. White tracksuit. Car keys in his hand. Frowning. Mad. He looked up and saw me coming.

I'd do him right there on the doorstep. Bare hands. Bring the whole shithouse down. Let Paterson pick up the pieces.

Raz stood there, filling the doorway. He squared his shoulders and pointed at me. Spoke low and husky with anger.

"Where you been?"

I didn't answer. I pounded up the path towards him, my hands twitching. Raz raised his voice.

"I told you we had to make it back for ten. You just bunked off and left us all?"

He stepped down onto the path. Mossie came up behind him in the doorway. Shovelling pot noodles in his gob. Do him too, then, would I? Fine. Almost there now. Four paces away. Two.

There was a sound. They turned to look behind them.

Hanzi was stood there in the hall. He muttered something and rubbed his eyes.

Raz growled at him to get back upstairs. Mossie raised his hand at the boy. Hanzi moved back a step and then stopped. Stood there. Didn't turn away. Stared up at Mossie.

I was meant to be dancing on the big man's corpse by now. Change of plan though, eh. Do Hanzi a favour for once. Don't make him watch a murder. I bought some time to sort my head out.

"It's alright Raz," I said. "I'll take him up."

They stared at me. No more killing that night then. More acting instead. More bullshit.

"Raz, mate. Mossie. I'm so sorry," I said. My honest Scouser act. Trying to laugh and clown around, never mind the din in my head. "I couldn't walk back with you. I saw this bird I know, Linzi."

Not much of a plan, was it. Owning up that I'd let him down at the first sniff of muff. Best I could come up with though.

They were staring at me still.

"I'm sorry," I said again. "Raz, mate. I messed up."

Raz narrowed his eyes. Didn't know what to make of it. He looked me up and down. Oil and mud on my trackie bottoms.

"We was copping off in the trees," I said. "It's well manky."

"And?"

"I'll see her next Sunday, if you don't need me."

Cheeky twat, me. Still. I'd chosen my story. All or nothing.

Raz raised his eyebrows and thought to himself for a sec. Mossie chewed his noodles, glaring at me. Shaking his head.

"What?" I stared Mossie out over Raz's shoulder. "Did you

have a hot date lined up too, did you? That'd be a first. Not seen many birds round here."

I gave Mossie a smirk and threw a glance up towards the lads' bedrooms. So he knew what I meant alright. Now he'd have to start on me or let it go.

"What?" I said again, still frowning at Mossie. "Not much shagging at your meetings either is there? It was either here or the Boy Scouts, eh?"

Raz turned on me. Gone too far, had I? Fight instead? Fine.

I braced myself, rocking lightly on the balls of my feet. But Raz was too fast. A swish of his arm, and my neck was in his hand. Choking. Crippling. His thumb digging up under my jaw. Perfect grip. He didn't squeeze, just held me there. His huge green eyes glaring into mine. Searching for something. Looking for lies.

I felt my feet leave the ground.

I gurgled and tried to swallow. Couldn't. I reached up with both hands and gripped his arm. Steel bar.

He held me there, dangling like a dead cat from his one hand. He shifted on his feet so the porch light shone on my face. Looking in my eyes the whole time.

The blood was churning up into my head. My skull felt like it'd pop open. My eyes straining out of their holes. Somehow I held his gaze. Kept up the act.

"Fuckin' come 'ead, then," I gurgled.

I'd almost passed out when he let me down. I dropped to my hands and knees, coughing and spluttering. Waited for the clouds to clear from my eyes. Tottered to my feet.

I stepped away from Raz and gave him a narky stare, holding my throat. Walked round on the path in a little circle, with tight, sulky paces, trying to cool off. Sparked up a Regal. Got to keep up the act, eh. That was why he hired me after all. For better or worse. Angry, randy, scrappy. He'd not want me to change.

My breath came back. Calmer. I didn't speak. Waited for Raz to.

Whatever he was looking for in my face, he had found it. He waved me into the house.

I stepped past them both. Mossie scowled at me and slurped his noodles. Hanzi was still stood there, watching. His little black eyes staring me out. I took his hand. My thoughts back in my head where they belonged. Not in my fists. My heartbeat eased.

I took Hanzi in the kitchen and made him a hot Ribena. Followed him upstairs and sat with him as he lay under the Spiderman cover, drinking. The Manc snoring in the next bed.

I talked to Hanzi in a low voice. Didn't know how much he understood, but I kept gobbing. It calmed me down.

I told him about Ali and Frank. The Grace. Then about my dad. I went on and on. I told Hanzi not to worry. I'd see he got looked after. He seemed to understand. I was still spouting as he drifted off.

I climbed the ladder to my attic. Felt the weight of the dead lad's phone in my pocket, knocking against my hip as I went. I took it out, wrapped it in a pair of pants and stashed it under my bed.

I crawled under the duvet. Freaked, knackered. As the sleep came, so did the dread.

Nightmares. I was running to catch a train but it was getting faster and faster away. My dad was on it. His three-stripe and muzzy. He stretched his arms out to haul me in but I couldn't reach him. Couldn't see his face, like always. A blur with floppy back hair and moustache. He drifted away, and the bodies of dozens of Hanzis crunched under the train wheels.

Chapter Nineteen

My eyes weren't open yet, but my mind and body had woken up. Legs and arms aching. Scratches and bruises on my arse. I knew I was in my bed in Raz's house. And I knew what I'd done.

The skylight was right over my head. No blind on it. Sun right on my eyelids. I rolled over and faced the bedside table.

Cup of tea on it.

I sat up with a jerk and looked around. No one there.

Raz? Or one of the lads? First time it had happened since I'd been here. And I hadn't done much to earn a favour.

My throat was all dry so I sat up and tried it. Stewy and strong. I sat and drank it and thought about what to do.

I was going down, now Paterson had dropped me. I saw what happened. He knew about Ali. Knew I'd broke the deal. And now I'd killed. Again. He'd haul me in. But he'd not come to the house to get me, would he. That'd give him away to Raz. The house was the safest place for me.

I needed a piss so I got up and creaked down the ladder in my boxies. I was late up. No one about on the landing. I listened. Heard voices downstairs. Clink of dishes. The lads in the kitchen having their Coco Pops.

I plodded across to the bathroom. No lock on the door. I knocked once and pushed it open.

She was sitting there on the toilet with the lid down.

The new one.

Bare feet with red toenails. Light blue Kappa trackie bottoms, white vest, no bra. Hair all wet, hiding her face as she leaned over to the mat at her feet, fiddling with something.

I didn't say nothing. I peered at her, trying to see what she'd got there. An old red biscuit tin. She pressed the lid down on it and slipped it behind the toilet bowl. Straightened up and flicked her hair back.

These big nutty dark eyes. Thin nose with a crystal stud.

87

Thin face. Her jaw moving, chewing gum clicking round in her mouth.

She gave me this dirty grin, like she'd known I was coming.

"I thought you was never waking up," she said. "Thought your tea would get cold."

"The tea," I said. "Ta."

"You're welcome."

She sat there on the toilet lid, stretched her toes out and looked at the nail paint.

"Can I have a biscuit with it?" I said.

"Why would I give you a biscuit?"

"For my blood sugar."

"I've not got any biscuits."

Soft husky Scouse voice. This sad drag to it.

"What's in the tin then?" I said.

"Trouble."

"Not a very good dinner lady, are you?"

"I'm not a dinner lady. That was a favour I did you. Raz said I'm not meant to go up to the lads' rooms unless I'm tidying them. And I'm never to go up to yours."

"Guess I owe you one, eh?"

"Nah, you're alright."

"Well do yourself a favour, then. Don't take Raz for granted like that."

She rolled her eyes. "Do you mind?" she said. "I was about to have a dump."

"Well, wash your hands before you make my breakfast."

"Why? Don't you like girls when they're dirty?"

She wrinkled her nose in a smile and snapped away at the chewy with her mouth open. I looked away. At the window, at the floor. I got my tongue back and spoke again.

"You living here now?" I said.

"Raz put me in the room across the hall from his. I got here last night."

"From where?"

"Not far."

She bit her lip. Little cut on it. These grey tired rings round her eyes. She pulled her feet up on the bog lid, folded her knees to her chest.

I opened my mouth. But before the words came out, she said: "Maya."

"Azo."

She smiled.

"Azo. You want to look in my biscuit tin?"

"I'm meant to be the Big Brother round here. Meant to know all what goes on."

She reached a skinny arm behind the bowl, pulled out the tin and held it out to me. She had that red paint on her fingernails too.

I stepped forward and took it. Old metal thing, with a hinged lid. Tartan pattern. Shortbread. I stretched my fingers and thumbs round it and worked it open.

Half an inch deep of skunk, wrapped in a plastic bag. Two packs of king size Rizlies on top. And her morning's work: a spliff.

"This my breakfast?" I said.

She smirked. "Fuck off."

I stuck my nose in. Almost got chonged off the smell. "What would Raz say if he saw this?" I said.

"He'd kill me."

She laughed again. A chuckle that shook her chest and shoulders and rolled on into a wheeze and a cough.

"Does Raz know you smoke?" I said.

"Knows I used to."

She licked the cut by her mouth. I pointed at it.

"Did Raz do that?"

"No," she said. "Raz helped me out."

"Where did he find you?"

"Mossie found me. Online."

"Asian bride?"

"Not that kind of site."

"Oh, I *see*." I mimed mouse-clicking and whacking off at the same time. I'm a real gent, me.

"Fuck off." She giggled. "The kind of site that doesn't show up in searches. The kind for real people."

"You a believer?" I said.

89

She shrugged. "I was brought up one. I'm enough of one to make everyone in that web forum like me. That's why Mossie picked me up."

"You don't talk like one."

"There's lots of ways of believing."

"So why did you… "

A noise came from downstairs. Raz, bellowing my name, then hers. Maya jumped up from the bog, hugged herself and looked at the door.

"He's in the hall," she said, and glanced at the biscuit tin in my hand. "What are we going to do with that?"

"Don't ask me. How did you get it up here?"

"Wrapped it in my towel."

"Well then."

"My towel's wet now. Raz said I've got to leave it on the rail."

"That was clever."

I knew what she was waiting for. Wanted me to play the gent and hide it for her. I took my time. Leaned my back against the door.

"I never knew Raz was so house proud," I said.

"I bet there's a lot about him you don't know."

"And you do?"

She shrugged. "There's a lot you don't know about me too."

I looked down at the biscuit tin and back at Maya. She winked at me, her jaw pounding the chewy. Something about her. I couldn't put on my act the way I did with Raz and the others. I felt like she could see right through me.

I muttered and looked at the biscuit tin. She stepped towards me. I smelt her clean wet hair. Downstairs Raz bellowed my name again.

"Can I not stash it in your room?" she said. "Just till tonight."

Maybe she was setting me up. Was Raz making her do it? Testing me after last night? While I was trying to think, he shouted again.

I'd take a chance. Get her on my side. I stepped away from the door.

"My hero," she said.

Her chest grazed my arm as she passed. Nuke charge through my whole body. I heard the lads whooping downstairs.

I nipped back up the ladder and stashed the biscuit tin on a beam in the attic ceiling. I scrambled some clothes on, had a quick piss and went down. The lads were sitting waiting in the back room.

Raz was standing in the kichen in a green basketball vest, finishing his coffee.

"No hurry, la'," he said.

"Sorry, Raz mate."

He was frowning, wondering what had got into me. I should have been on my best behaviour after that fuckup the night before. I stayed cool. Didn't go crawling to him. One sorry and that'd do. Cool things down while I had a think what to do.

Raz thought for a second, sniffed and let it go.

"You take the lads out the back," he said. "Give them some of your training. Teach them how to stay alive!"

I grabbed a banana and a Penguin bar from the worktop. Stuffed the bicky in my gob as I zipped my coat up and put the banana in my pocket.

As I was heading out the kitchen, Maya came through. She looked at me as we edged past each other in the doorway, face to face. My mouth was full of chocky biscuit.

I ordered the lads out the back. Spitting with rain it was. They grumbled. I raised my voice and they tramped out, through the little washing room off the kitchen, to the back door. Only Rodney lingered there in the sitting room, staring at the telly.

"And you," I said.

He turned and stared at me. I pulled him out of his chair, kicked him up the arse and shoved him in the back.

He turned and gave me a look.

"Got something to say?" I growled.

I held his eye. Two seconds. Three. He snorted, slouched out and strutted down the back steps.

I was about to follow him down when I heard Maya and Raz talking low in the kitchen. The door was open a crack. I peered through.

She was standing at the table in front of him. He got a key from his trackie pocket, turned and unlocked one of the upper cupboards. Took out three little boxes. White ones from the chemist with printed labels. He popped capsules out of their plastic bubbles into his palm and laid them on the table.

He handed her a glass of water and grabbed her chin. Her cheek turned white under his fingers. He slotted the pills in her gob one by one, held the glass to her lips and watched her as she swallowed.

He locked the packets back in the cupboard and pocketed the key.

Outside I had the lads pull the gym mats out the garden shed and lay them on the lawn. I stuffed the banana down me for strength. Didn't enjoy it. Didn't feel hungry. Felt sick. I couldn't taste. Couldn't think.

Afraid someone'd come for me. Paterson would hear about the lad on the tracks and send his pigs to haul me in.

Teach the lads some moves, Raz had told me. Teach them what you learned at that boxing ring.

I did my best. Slapped Casho and Manc Lee round the head to calm them down. I had them all stand round and watch while I taught them some bits and pieces. Falling, ducking, blocking. Wrist-, arm- and neck-locks. I made the lads run through the moves with me, one by one, then pair off and try them on each other. Gently.

I finished up by showing them that wicked neck-pinch. I took Rodney as a guinea pig. The cocky knobhead was well into stepping up for a demo. He hopped around on the mat, clucking away like Bruce Lee. He shut up quick when my fingers reached his throat. His knees buckled. Down he went on his back.

I looked at the lads over my shoulder. They shut up and stood there watching.

"This'll kill him if I squeeze hard enough," I told them.

Turned and grinned down at Rodney. His eyes were buggling. "Don't try it at home," I told him. "Oops, I forgot. This is your home now, isn't it?"

A voice came from the kitchen step. Raz.

I eased my grip on Rodney's neck. He spluttered and gasped and rolled over panting. He lay there on his side for a bit then slowly got to his knees.

Raz called out again. Mossie had come, he told me. School time for the lads.

I had them put the mats away, then file up the back steps one by one. Me last and Rodney in front, still panting. He avoided my eye. Raz stood at the door and saw them through into the sitting room.

Mossie was sat there on a stool, waiting with his back to the telly. He had his white pyjama-suit on with a trackie top over it. Slippers on his feet. Book on his lap. Rodney leaned over as he came in, reached for Mossie's book and turned it up to see the cover. Mossie wrenched it away from him and pointed him to one of the chairs.

The lads settled down around him. I sat off behind them on a kitchen chair. The vacuum cleaner was whirring upstairs. Maya had set out cups of tea and plates of fig rolls on the coffee table. The lads scoffed the bickies and left the steaming tea to cool.

Raz came in from the kitchen and closed the door behind him. They twisted their heads round as he stood and spoke to them from behind the settee.

"Learning to fight, lads? Top stuff. God knows you've had a lot taken from you. Lot of fighting to do to get it back."

"With God's help," Rodney said, through a mouthful of fig roll. He was sitting there slumped in the settee, holding a biscuit in one hand and rubbing his neck with the other.

Raz pointed at him and nodded, frowning. "Right on, la'," he said. "That's why we're here. This house gives back to you lads everything that this country has taken from you. Raz give you food and shelter. Azo give you power to fight. Now Mossie give you the third pillar. The dearest of all. He give you back your soul."

Book-bashing class with Mossie, eh. This should be a laugh.

I didn't get to sit in, though. Raz headed out into the hall and beckoned me to come with him. I heard Mossie's wool drawl start up. Raz shut the sitting-room door behind him and stood with his back to it.

He planted a hand on my shoulder.

"I'm taking the lads to Warrington this evening," he told me. "What for?"

His eyes sparkled. "See a teacher who'll show them the way. These lads know they have to fight. Our wise man teach them just why."

"Who is this feller?"

He gave a tight smile. "You're not coming," he told me. "You're driving to Tranmere with Casho and Ayax."

"The oil dock?"

"Right, la'. There's a big jolly ship stopping there tonight. Jolly sailor on board got something for me."

He held up a hand for me to wait and went in his room, closing the door behind him. I heard him rummaging in a drawer. He came out again with a white envelope in one hand and something black in the other.

"This is for the jolly sailor," he said, passing me the envelope. "He give you the goodies."

"What goodies?"

He winked. "Pressie from my friends in Monrovia. My man be looking out for you near the gate."

"It'll be guarded."

"You'd be amazed, la'. My man's a very clever man."

"Bloody hell. Alright."

"Then you got another stop to make. On your way back."

He handed me a slip of paper with an address. Unit number. Some warehouse off Derby Road.

"Another jolly ship docked at Seaforth. Something else for me. Pressie from my chums in Tirana. Truck driver's going to park it up in the depot. Casho and Ayax help you load it in the car."

Another envelope.

"This is for the driver. From Raz, you tell him."

"I'll take the Astra, then?"

He shook his head.

"The Mazda."

"The what?"

"Old car. But a goodie." He took a key out of his pocket. "Just for tonight, lad. Anything go wrong, that souped-up Chitty-Bang'll get you out of there quickie-quick, la'. Then you dump it. No one trace. It's parked outside."

I breathed deep and held down the sickness in my gut.

Late afternoon, Raz took the other lads to get the train. Me and Casho and Ayax stayed home and headed out at dusk.

Chapter Twenty

It was a bit rattly and dusty but it ran fine. I drove it down to the main road, turned right and peeled off the roundabout towards the big set of lights. When they turned green we shot off along Hawthorne Road.

Past the gutted warehouses I turned at the old pub and drove along Linacre Road, towards the winking lights on the derricks. Good old Bootle docks. We were going beyond them this time, though, to the other side of the river.

We had a clear run down to the Queensway tunnel. Last time I'd been over the river was with Leanne three summers back. She'd had some auntie there or something. I couldn't remember much about it. I was speeding my bollocks off that day. But I know we took the ferry. Leanne was a soppy cow back then. We'd stood and snogged on the deck.

This time I went under the river. We came out in Birkenhead and took this dingy road towards the oil terminal. Half a mile along there was a turnoff to the left by a locked gate.

We got out. I told Casho and Ayax to keep an eye up and down the road. Someone had left a load of pallets stacked up there. I clambered up them and stood at the top for a view to the river. Liverpool on the far side, all sprinkled with lights. And on the near bank, a few hundred yards south, the fat round tanks of the oil dock.

A ship was moored at the north jetty with its arse towards me. Long and black with a red hull, lit up by blazing yellow lights on the pier.

I strained my eyes to read the writing on the back.

"Monrovia. That where it's from?"

Standing down there in the dark, Casho heard me. "Liberia," he said. "That where it's flag from. The ship could sail from anywhere."

I climbed back down the stack. We all got back in the car.

"How do we get in there then?" Ayax asked as I started the

engine.

"We can't."

I palmed the Mazda out of the lay-by and crept along another half-mile. Signs pointed off left for the way in to the dock. We skirted a wall with barbed wire on the top and saw the entry straight ahead. Double yellows all along the road to a grey steel gate. Beyond it, the big white tubs, yellow cranes looming and lights twinkling on the ships.

No sign of Raz's man, whoever he was. To the left of the gate stood a little red-brick house for the guards. No way I was hanging around there.

I crunched through a three-point turn and drove back up to the main road.

I spotted something in the rearview as I went. Walking along behind us going the same way, heading off from the terminal gate. A feller in a grey hoodie.

I slowed down and let him get closer. Just round the bend, I stopped. The feller turned and looked at me as he walked past. I got a glimpse of a young pale face. Little string rucksack on his back. He seemed to nod under his hood and wagged the tips of his fingers at his mouth like he wanted to eat something. He pointed up the road. I drove off slow, keeping him in the mirror.

There was a drive-thru KFC just over the dual carriageway across from the dock. I pulled up in its car park with the nose of the Mazda pointing north. I unclipped my seatbelt, rolled down my window and sparked up a ciggie while we waited for the hoodie lad to catch up.

Casho asked if he could go in the KFC to get a drink. Okay, I said. I could use a sip myself. My mouth was well dry. It was one of them weird English summer nights when the air smells all foreign.

I looked in the rearview. Four lads were sitting on the far side of the car park with KFC bags and bottles. Pissed-up, dicking around. Flicking hot rags of chicken batter and sloshing each other with cider. Cackling and swearing.

The hoodie lad took a while to cross the carriageway and make it round to the KFC. After a few minutes he popped up at the way in to the car park. He saw the Mazda, stopped and glanced around him. I waited. He looked like he was about to walk towards us. Just then Casho came back out through the sliding door, a paper cup in his hand. He loped across the car park towards us under the street lights.

I turned to watch him. As he reached the car, he slowed his step and looked behind him. He'd heard something. I heard it too, through the crack in my window.

A voice from the far side.

"'Ey, mate. 'Scuse me lad, 'ey. Have you got any Rizlies there mate?"

Casho didn't understand. He stopped and looked at me, then behind him at the group of lads. He shook his head without a word and walked on.

"'Ey, lad. I'm talkin' to you."

The back door handle clicked on my side as Casho reached it. He was halfway in when one of the cider lads showed. This boss trackie he had, all black with the red, green and gold three-stripes down it. Big and lanky with boned short hair. His eyes were blurry and grumpy. His voice tightened a notch as he spoke again.

I turned the key.

"'Ey, lad. D'you speak English?"

He ran towards us as Casho slipped in and slammed the door shut. I glanced left. Another scrote had shown up on that side.

I felt the sliding clunks behind me as Casho and Ayax locked their doors. I let the handbrake down and reached for my lock a second late. My door opened.

"'Ey, lad. Tell your mate I wanna talk to him."

"We've got no Rizlies, mate. I'm sorry."

"I just wanna talk to him."

I tried to reach for the door to pull it shut. Tricky with one foot braced on the clutch. I glanced over to the way out. The hoodie lad was gone.

Three-stripe held me back in my seat and tightened his grip on my shoulder.

"Hang on, lad," he said. "I'm talkin' to you."

"Leave it out, mate."

"Get out."

His mate had opened the door on the pavement side. He leaned in and looked up at me. Blond lad with freckles.

"'Ey, lad," he said. "Where you goin'?"

I heard Paterson's voice in my head, reminding me what my job was. Guard your country, Azo. Britain. Your own folk, your freedoms, your way of life. Guard it all, for better or worse, or all that's left is mayhem.

The other two lads had come and were leaning on the bonnet. They scattered and yelled when the Mazda started to roll. The lanky one leaning in my door hopped along with his foot inside on my seat.

Our hoodie lad had shown up again, across from us on the far side of the turnoff. I saw him duck down behind a parked car. Then I saw what had made him run. Someone else had shown up at the car park entry. Stocky, bald feller. White shirt under his vest, black trousers and boots. A guard from the dock.

He clocked the Mazda. He was looking around him for the hoodie lad.

I jigged out the clutch and let the car jerk forward faster. The big lad held on, hopping along with me. He wasn't going away. I'd have to find a way to make him useful.

"Come 'ead then, you big fanny," I said. "We'll take the lot of you."

I rammed the gas and churned the clutch out. The wheels crackled as the Mazda lurched forward. The freckly lad on my left side crumpled, slipped to the tarmac and fell away. The door pranged to but wouldn't shut as I zipped towards the way out. The lad in the black trackie gripped my arm. I ground it up to twenty. He tripped away and rolled into the gutter.

A little way down the road, I did a U-ey and headed back towards them. I braked as we got close.

"What you doing, Azo?" Ayax yelled. "Fast now!"

"Hang on."

I squeaked to a halt just across from the KFC, near the car where I'd seen the hoodie duck down. The four cider lads were standing yelling at the site guard.

"You two get out and have them," I said.

"Azo, you crazy?" yelled Ayax. "Man is here."

"Remember what I've taught you."

I left the Mazda running and climbed out. I raised my arms at the cider lads.

"Come 'ead then," I yelled.

As Casho and Ayax loped across the road, I scuttled round and crouched behind the car.

The guard shouted. My lads laid into the scalls. I'd taught them well. No one was looking at me. I crept away behind the cars.

The hoodie lad was crouching a few yards down, trying to watch the scrap through a car window. He jumped when he saw me. I put my finger to my lips. I took the first envelope out of my top and held it up as I crept towards him.

"Raz says hi."

He slipped the little rucksack off his back and handed it over. I took hold of the draw-strings with one hand and lifted. Twenty pounds it must have weighed.

"What's your name, lad?" I said.

He stared at me. Spotty, pasty lad with pale blue eyes. He said nothing.

I loosened the strings and looked in the bag. This little grey steel box in there. Raz hadn't told me what I was looking for. No time to chat about it though. Casho and Ayax were yelling. I handed the envelope to the lad. He took it, looked inside, then at me, and stuck it down his top. He glanced over his shoulder and sprinted off back towards the Rock Ferry Bypass.

I stood up and watched. The guard never saw him go. He was stooping over one of the cider lads in the gutter, trying to give him first aid. One of the lad's mates lay near him. The other two had run off.

Casho and Ayax were getting back in the Mazda. I was scrambling in behind the wheel, shoving the rucksack onto the passenger seat, when something gripped my shoulder. My big pal from before, in the boss trackie.

I shoved him off and he reeled back but didn't fall. I stepped out of the car.

It all went quiet and still in my head. I stood and watched him strut towards me. I picked out a spot on him. The middle of his lips where his yellow ratty teeth showed.

I left him lying for the guard to nurse.

I smiled to myself. My day's work was almost over. Soon we were squealing back up towards Birkenhead. The tunnel. Bootle. Just one more stop. No trouble this time. A dark depot in among the warehouses off the dock road. A quiet driver who hardly spoke English. A metal carry-crate. I gave him his envelope while the hefted it into the boot.

I dropped them with the bag and the box at our front gate, drove off and dumped the car where Raz told me, on a waste ground the far side of Rimrose Valley. On the walk back, I ducked into a kiddies' playground, found a bench and sat hunched over on it. I got my phone out and tried to call Paterson. He didn't pick up. Too bad for him, that dickhead. He'd have loved to hear about all this.

Chapter Twenty-One

I gave Maya a leg-up through the skylight where the attic roof sloped. Her bare foot with them painted toenails, cradled in my hand. Her arse packed in her tight Kappa bottoms. Biscuit tin in her left hand.

Being with her calmed me well down. The smoky smell of her and the sound of her voice, all warm and hopeless at the same time. Up she went and scrambled out of sight, sniggering and swearing under her breath.

I pulled myself up after her and poked my head through the skylight. She'd slid down the tiles to the bottom where a bit of the roof of the downstairs bedroom jutted out flat. Rodney was asleep in the room below.

I came slipping down the slates and settled next to her on the flat bit.

We looked out over the rooftops. Clear black summer sky. Stars. Porch lights. Buzz of traffic on Church Road. And from far down on the ground floor, the rumble of Raz snoring.

She opened her tin and rustled around in it, skinning up. She must have already smoked that first one in the afternoon. She peeled off a bunch of Rizlies, licked them up and started patching them together and sprinkling in tobacco and skunk leaves. More licking. In no time she had it rolled fat and tight. Sparked it up and sucked off that bitter first gobful. She coughed on the smoke, pulled again, deeper, and held it in.

I looked at her face in the glow as she tugged a third time. Wrinkles went out of her forehead. Her shiny sad eyes misted over. Little smile on her face. She let the smoke out slowly. Took another long lungful and handed the spliff to me.

"You trying to get me fired?" I said.

"Yeah."

I held in my first drag deep and long. Wondered if she was going to talk. She didn't. She wrapped her arms round her knees and shut her eyes. I opened my mouth at last and blew the smoke off over the rooftops towards Seaforth. That grassy taste as it rolled out my nose. I could already feel the tingling in my fingers and toes.

"Where did you get this?" I said.

"Stole it before I came here."

I took a second pull. My legs went numb. "Who from?"

"My ex."

I coughed and spluttered out the smoke.

"Don't worry. He'll not come looking for me," she said. "He'd have to deal with Raz."

My third lungful. I held it in a while. Felt happier. Started to forget about everything. I let the smoke out. My voice came out all strangled with it.

"You and Raz?" I said.

She opened her eyes. "He wishes. He come to my room last night after lights out. Sat on my bed. Talked."

"What about?"

"Same stuff he tells the lads. Right and wrong. The past. Wars. Says I've got my own role to play. He's got something planned for me."

"What did you say?"

"Nothing. Just listened. Squeezed his hand. Waited for him to go."

"So why is he giving you the pills?"

She stared out over the rooftops like she'd not heard. I said it again. My voice came from far away. "The pills," I said. "I saw you this morning."

"I have to take them. With the lads around, he keeps them locked up."

"What happens if you stop?"

"I get bad."

"Why?"

"No reason."

She took back the spliff.

"Won't this mess you up then?" I said.

She gave a hopeless shrug and stared at the sky. Shrinking back into her own world, where you couldn't reach her. Where her eyes didn't see you. Just like my mum. It drove me nuts,

103

that look. Made me sad. Made me want her more. That and the skunk, eh. I'd only had three tugs and I was well stoned. Feeling all soft.

"So how did you get here? I said. It came out sounding all deep. "I mean what are you here for? I mean what happened? Where's your folks?"

"Formby."

"You a bit posh?"

She shrugged. "Not been home for a while. Not since I lost my job."

"Job, eh? You get flasher and flasher, you. Job where?"

"Bank."

I spluttered. "You blagging?"

"No. It went tits up with all the others."

She rolled over on her side towards me, looking me in the eyes as she blew her smoke in my face.

"So you've got folks but you never see them?" I said.

"I see my mum. Sometimes."

"Wish I had a mum in Formby," I said. "Wish I had any folks at all. Only wanted a quiet life, me. Home. Garden. Sofa and an X-Box."

I was talking too much. Found myself telling her about Ali. Frank. Leanne. Barely managed to keep my mouth shut about Paterson.

She curled up next to me and patted my arm.

"So what's Raz got planned for you?" I said.

"Don't know. I'll not stick around long enough to find out."

"Why not?"

"I've got something planned for him first."

Chapter Twenty-Two

I still hadn't got to see what was in those boxes. Raz had me busy running the house. Coco Pops for brekkie each morning, then training out the back. I taught the lads and Maya how to block and hold and hit. Crunch, snap, throttle. How to kill, stuff like that. Easy. Top use of taxpayers' money, that training. It had sorted me out. Now I was sharing it with other young people. It helped me pass the time till I was up on the roof with her again.

"So come on, then. What's this plan of yours?"

It was the night after our first spliff-off.

"Eh?" she said, blowing out a lungful. I couldn't tell if she was really dopey or just making like she was.

"For Raz."

If she was going to stir things up, I wanted to get it moving. Raz had been cold on me ever since that night when I went down to the tracks. If he sussed out who I was, he'd take me down in the cellar.

Maya rolled her head round on the slates to face me and passed me what was left of the spliff.

"You found out what's in that crate yet?" she said.

"Course not. No one can get into Raz's room. If you did, he'd kill you."

"Don't you want to know what's in it?"

"Course I do. I nearly got done nicking the thing."

"Time we searched his room then."

I sat and took that in. I'd thought of that when I first come to the house. I'd reckoned it was too risky to try breaking in. I'd told myself I'd look for a chance and put it to the back of my mind. Search his room. It was the first thing I should have done.

"Even if you did get in," I said, "the box is locked."

"Next you'll be telling me you there's a password to read his mails."

"He doesn't do email."

"Really? He does a lot of typing behind that door."

What could I say? I'd had a lot on my mind since I'd started in the house. Hadn't had time for any fancy crap like listening at doors.

"Well, yeah then. It will have a password."

"Never stopped me."

I sat there with the spliff in my hand, looking at her with my mouth open like a div.

She smiled. "Come on, Azo. You don't look like the kind of lad who'd let a locked door get in his way."

"You're dangerous."

"You love it."

"I wouldn't if Raz caught me in his sock drawer."

"Fuck socks. I'm getting in his PC."

More to this bird than I thought then, eh. Well, well. Part of my job. Some day I'd have to get to the bottom of who she was and what she knew. But just then she was moving too fast. All I could do was cling on.

"Hack him?" I said. "You know how to do that?"

"My ex taught me."

"And where's he? In Formby?"

"No. He's left."

"Where to?"

"Syria."

I took a deep breath. "So you hack the big man. Then what?"

She grabbed the spliff back and brushed a scrap of ash off the front of my t-shirt. Her fingertips grazed my right pec. She stuck the spliff in her gob and winked at me.

Raz's bedroom door had a shiny new Yale lock. A night latch on the inside by the look of it. You could usually open them with a bit of jigging and strength and a stiff sheet of sandpaper. Jenks had shown us how in the posh jail. But unless you're a right pro it scratches up the lock and the door frame. I'd had half a day on it with Jenks but I'd never tried it for myself on the outside. Raz would see straightaway that one of us had messed with his door.

Jenks had been going to teach me how to pick locks for real, fiddling about in them with pins and stuff. I'd been looking forward to that. But then Paterson had called me in that day without warning and sent me straight out to Toxteth. I'd not seen Jenks again.

I warned Maya about all that, to stop her diving straight in and messing it up. She was in a hurry alright. I talked her into waiting a day or two so we could work something out.

"What about Manc Lee?" she said.

She was right. I remembered his life story from that rainy day down by the docks.

Maya had heard it too.

"He told everyone he knows how to pick locks," she said.

"Raz will know it's him, then, won't he?"

"Raz will never find out. We'll pick the lock, not force it."

"The Manc's shit-scared of Raz, like all of us. He'll never say yes."

"We'll make him."

We played cricket in the park again that evening. When we got back to the house, I asked the Manc to help me carry the bats and stumps out back.

At the bottom of the garden, I opened the shed door and he went in and put his stumps down. As I stepped in after him, I felt a hand on my shoulder. Maya had snuck up on us. She followed me in. We stood there all three in the tight space between the door and the stack of mats and junk.

"Alright?" said the Manc.

We didn't have much time. Raz was in the kitchen tossing pancakes. I told the Manc Raz was going out the next afternoon to see his man in Warrington. Told him what he had to do.

"You off your trolley?" he said. "He'll rip my head off."

"Not if he doesn't find out."

"What do you care what's in his room?" he said.

Maya put her hand on my arm and squeezed past me. She stood close to the Manc.

"Lee, love. It's not safe here," she said.

"Not with you around."

"I know you're scared of Raz. We're all scared. That's why you've got to help us."

He looked suss. "Not safe how?" he said.

"He's planning something," she said.

"Like what?"

"We don't know. That's why we've got to get in his room. To find out."

He still looked suss. "I'm doing alright here. Better than on the street."

I heard a clink of plates from the kitchen. Raz would be calling us in soon.

"You'd be better on the street than dead," I said.

He looked at me. Worried now. He believed I was one of Raz's main men. And he believed I was turning against him.

"I mean it," I said. "He doesn't care about us. He's using us. And it's going to end bad."

"Raz has said he'll sort us out," the Manc said. "Why should I trust you?"

I shrugged. "No good reason," I said. "But we're having a go at his bedroom door tomorrow. If we mess it up because you won't help, we'll tell him you were with us anyway. I reckon he'd believe us. Everyone knows you're the burglar in this house."

I was sorry to put the screws on the Manc like that. He was alright, Lee. But I had to work quick. Raz had his eye on us. Most of all me. Every minute we spent plotting out there in the shed meant more risk.

The Manc looked down at his trainies. He didn't know what to say. I was about to start bullying him into it, but Maya spoke again. Her soppy breathy voice.

"At least do it for Hanzi, love," she said. "Raz's got it in for us all. Little Hanzi hasn't done nothing."

He met her eye and nodded.

That night on the roof, me and Maya patted each other on the back about getting the Manc on board.

"You not scared of messing with Raz?" I asked her.

She shook her head. I couldn't tell if she was faking. She

had that faraway look in her eyes.

"Long as he keeps giving me my pills, I'm safe in here," she said. "I'll find out what he's up to. I'll get a piece of him."

"I reckon he'd like a piece of you."

She grabbed the biscuit tin and twatted me round the head with it. She giggled at the look on my face. Twatted me again.

I grabbed the tin and tried to get it off her. Braced my back against the sloping roof. The two of us trying not to laugh. She wouldn't let go. I pulled harder, dragging her towards me. She steadied herself. Swung her leg over me and sat in my lap.

Shiny stud she had, in her belly where the top rode up. She let go of the tin. Me too. I let it drop by my side. She put a hand to the back of my head and grabbed a fistful of hair and scalp. Jerked it back and went deep in my mouth with her tongue.

I wanted to eat her up in gobfuls. But she slowed me down. Hushed me so we wouldn't wake the others. The quiet and the dark. Them fizzy orange street lights winking off the slate roofs all across north Liverpool. The swish of cars on Church Road. Her sweet skin, nose stud, belly. Our cloudy eyes clearing as we touched each other.

Chapter Twenty-Three

Next afternoon Raz and Mossie went out to Warrington. Told me to stay home and look after Maya and the lads.

I asked him who they were going to see. He just gave us his barmy look and pumped one of his fists like he was pulling a lever.

"Cherching!" he said. "All the fruit!"

"Someone rich?" I said. "One of Mossie's mates?"

"Pay unto Caesar," Raz said, winking at me.

"Right."

"Never mind the ins and outs, la'," he said. "You keep showing the lads the way of the dragon."

He put his arm round Mossie's neck, all matey, and dragged him out of the front door. He winked at me as they left. He didn't slap me on the back like he used to.

I made Rodney take the lads out to play cricket in the park. Stood on the doorstep smoking a fag as they went off down the road. I turned and stepped back into the hall. Maya was standing outside Raz's door. A minute later the Manc came back up the garden path.

He'd found some old crappy hacksaw blades in the shed, snapped one of them up into bits and ground away the teeth on a flagstone at the bottom of the garden. Then he'd shown me this springy metal pin thing he kept in his wallet.

He got on his knees and started frigging around in Raz's lock with the two bits of metal. He started off gently, but no luck. He got wound up and started swearing to himself. Tensing up. No good for teasing the lock.

After twenty minutes I put my hand on his shoulder.

"Alright, lad," I said. "Have a break, eh."

"I'm sorry, Azo, mate. I did my best."

"Forget it."

I patted the Manc on the shoulder and turned to look at Maya.

She was smiling, holding her phone.

"What?" I said.

She held it out to me. A photo of me and Lee on there. She swiped a finger across the touch-screen. More pics. Lee on his knees with his tools in Raz's lock and me kneeling watching.

She slipped the phone in her jeans pocket and pulled something out of it with the same hand. She held it up.

A silver Yale key.

"I nicked it out of Raz's pocket when he was giving me my pills. He leans in close."

The Manc stared at her.

"Give us that phone," he said.

"I'll wipe them off this one if you like," she said. She did it as I watched. "But I've already saved them to the cloud." She squeezed his arm. "Don't worry, love," she said. "I'll not show Raz nothing. But I will need your help. Both of you."

She moved towards the door. I grabbed the wrist of the hand with the key in it.

"There's no need for that," I said. "We're all in this together."

She tried to yank her hand free but I held it firm. She looked at me. "Raz comes to see me at night," she said. "We're not in that together, are we?"

"If he touches you, I'll have him."

"All these big strong men around, eh," she said. "A girl's got to be careful."

She shook my hand off. She stepped past us both and unlocked Raz's bedroom door.

The laptop was on a scratchy wooden desk in the far corner. Maya went straight to it while me and the Manc looked around the room. Not much to it. Bare floorboards. Single bed against the near wall with a rumpled duvet. Chest of drawers in front of the window. Little fridge in one corner.

Not much else. Old trainies on the floor. Newspapers and magazines stacked up by the bed. Nothing dodgy that I could see. Just a smell of socks.

On the inner wall, to our left as we came in, that big metal box we'd picked up in Bootle. The Manc kneeled down in front of it and started fiddling with his tools in the padlock.

I looked over at Maya in the far corner. She was sitting in the wooden chair at Raz's desk. She'd switched on his laptop. To try and get her back, I took a pic of her sitting there. Came out shit on my crappy Nokia though didn't it. Blurry photo of a girl at a desk. Could have been anywhere.

A pinboard hung on the wall behind her, all covered in maps. I went and stood next to Maya so I could look at them. She didn't look at me. I stared at the maps. They'd been ripped out of a big atlas.

Syria.

Most of the place names meant nothing to me. Someone'd drawn rings round ones in the shit-end of nowhere, miles from anything that looked like a town. I tried to store a few of them in my mind. I felt panic stirring in my belly. When Paterson had first stopped answering I was just mad at him. Now it was making me anxy. This was getting real. He needed to know about it.

I looked over my shoulder, down at Maya. Saw the desk had three drawers, to the left of her. I reached down and tried them. Locked, all three.

She'd tried to open the internet. Nothing. There was no wifi in Raz's house. Maya took her smartphone and switched on the wireless hotspot then got the laptop online through that.

She looked in the browsing history and found he'd used Hotmail. She opened it. There was his address saved in the login field.

"How's Raz get online without wifi?" I said.

"Same way I do, I guess. He's got a smartphone like me."

She looked up and grinned when she saw me watching her.

"I've never seen it," I said.

"He puts it on the bedside table at night."

I ground my teeth.

"Hey."

I looked across the room. The Manc was kneeling by the box, holding up the padlock in his hand.

I stood over his shoulder and watched as he lifted the lid.

I took them out gently, one by one. Half a dozen Glocks and

Sig Sauers. Half a dozen Klashnis. I counted them and laid them gently back in the box.

I looked around Raz's room. A lightbulb hung from the ceiling inside one of them paper globe shades. Not much else to see. Just them three locked drawers in the desk. And the fridge. I went over to look inside it.

It was locked an' all. Little silver keyhole at the top of the door.

A locked fridge.

I called the Manc over to come and have a go. He sighed and sat himself in front of it, fiddling away.

I looked over at Maya. She sat back in the chair with a grin. I went over to her and peered at the screen.

"You're joking," I said.

She'd got into Raz's mails.

The inbox was empty.

"Who's he writing to?" I said.

"Don't know," she said. "No sent mail. No saved mail. Nothing in the trash. Looks like he's scrubbed it all."

"Great."

"Hang on."

She clicked.

"There's something in the drafts."

A message. Just the one. Nothing in the 'to' field. Just an unsent mail. One line:

You tell us when. We tell our man in Raqqa. Peace mercy

I glanced behind me at the map. There it was near the top. Raqqa. That spod Lawrence had talked about it in the posh jail.

"So Raz knows a man in Syria," I said.

Maya stared at the screen a sec. Then she shook her head.

"Nah," she said. "Not Raz."

"What's he talking about then?"

She logged out of hotmail. Then she delved into his settings, wiping stuff to cover her tracks.

"Go on then," I said. "Why does he say he's got a man there?"

"Raz didn't write that."

"Right. Some other guy called Raz using this laptop."

"It's not signed Raz. It's not how he talks. It's his friends."

I was lost.

"Raz didn't write this," she said again. "Someone's written it for *him*. He's sharing this mail with his mates, whoever they are. They're saving drafts for each other to read."

"Why?"

"Less chance of getting traced if they're not sending them. They take it in turns to log in and read."

"You mean we've just hacked into the emails of a Syrian gang?"

Maya just smiled. She twitched her shoulders and straightened her back. She checked what web pages he'd been on. Nothing juicy. The only sites we found were BBC news and CNN. Outbreaks in Africa. Same old world going on out there. Same old shit footie teams. Same dirty fighting.

Maya pulled a memory stick out of her back pocket and stuck it in the side of Raz's laptop. I heard the Manc swear.

He couldn't get anywhere with that fridge lock.

I tried Paterson later, out on the roof. Didn't answer, did he. I lost it this time. Nearly lashed the phone off into the garden. Stopped myself. Reined it in.

This was too big. I couldn't get through it without Paterson. I saw that now. I needed him.

In the end I did it the old-fashioned way. I popped out to the post office. I scribbled a note about the guns and the mails. Didn't sign it or anything. I just stuck it in an envelope and mailed it to Paterson, care of Saint Anne's Street bizzies.

Chapter Twenty-Four

"How did you learn to fight like that then?" Rodney said.

Few days later. He was sitting in his dressing gown after a sesh on the mats. I'd given them bananas to use as knives. We were in the back room, waiting for the Manc to get out of the shower.

"My mate Frank," I said. "Taught me at his ring."

"Where?"

I didn't say nothing. Kicked myself. Wondered what Rodney'd ask next.

Maya came in and put a tray down on the coffee table. Tea and Jaffa Cakes. Rodney picked up a cup and slurped it. Stuffed a spongy Jaffa Cake in his gob. Fixed his eyes on Maya's arse as she straightened up.

She turned and handed me a cup. Caught my eye. Rodney glanced sideways at me and her standing there together. He'd seen how we looked at each other.

Maya was heading back to the kitchen when Raz came in. She halted in the doorway.

"Alright boss?" I said.

Raz fixed me with a frown.

"You was working in your room," I said. "So I took the lads out on the mats."

"I wasn't in my room, la'. I was in yours."

I felt my stomach turn over, thinking of the stash of weed.

"Why?" I said.

"Why not?"

He glared at me. His big bottom lip hanging open. Maya stood behind him, watching.

Raz reached in his combats, took something out and thrust it towards me. Little white thing.

I nearly threw up.

Worse than the weed, it was. The smartphone. The one from the lad on the tracks.

115

I'd forgot about it. Wrapped up in pants under my bed.

I heard Rodney munching behind me. Didn't know how he managed to make a noise chewing a fluffy Jaffa Cake. He was a gifted little shit.

I turned round and gave him a look. Lee called from the landing. Shower was free. Rodney swallowed and licked his lips. Picked up his bath towel and ponced upstairs.

I turned back to meet Raz's glare. Stayed calm, like I'd nothing to hide. Tried to think. It was only a phone. Didn't prove nothing.

I shrugged and looked Raz in the eye. "I don't know what to tell you, mate," I said. "It's a phone."

"It is, la'. But it's not your old Nokia, is it? One like this cost hundreds of quid in the shop. Where did you get it?"

I said nothing.

He pressed one of the keys and the screen lit up.

"I switched it on," Raz said. "Then someone called."

I started mapping out the house in my head. Living room door, hall. Front door, Chubb latch. Porch, doorstep. I sized up Raz as he loomed over me. Casho, Ayax and the Manc sitting around. Wondered what my chances were, if it came to it. Whether I'd get out in one piece.

"I answered it," Raz said. He stepped closer, his mad green eyes burning a hole in my head. I remembered the last time he'd got that close. He'd dangled me by the neck till I foamed at the gob.

"And?" I said.

"Someone told me I was a dead man. And hung up."

My heart was banging.

"Where did you get it?" he said again.

I opened my mouth to speak but Raz looked away. Down at his shoulder. Maya had laid her hand on it.

"Raz, love," I heard her say. Her face was hidden from me behind his huge bulk. "It's not his. It's mine."

I peered over his shoulder at Maya, frowning at her, shaking my head. She wouldn't meet my eye. She looked up at Raz instead. Flash of fear on her face for a second, then she hid it.

"I robbed it," she said.

116

"You what?"

"Last night. I went out for ciggies. Spotted it in this feller's pocket, in the queue at the garage."

Raz glanced back at me.

I should have spoken up. Couldn't let her take the shit for that. Never knew what Raz might do. Scared though, wasn't I. Losing my grip on this now. I kept my mouth shut. Tried not to tremble. Tried to think.

"Azo doesn't know anything about it," Maya said. "I stashed it in his room. I never told him."

Raz stepped towards her, flexing his knuckles. The floorboard creaked. I braced myself to grab him. I'd let him hit me instead. Let him try.

No need though. He swerved clear of Maya and punched the old door frame. Loosened a trickle of dust and plaster onto the floorboards.

"I told you all," he yelled. "No thieving, no fighting, no nothing unless I say. Or you'll have the pigs round."

Maya shrank back against the kitchen door. Her voice came out all soft. Pleading. Or faking it well. "I was going to show it you today. It's yours, love," she told him. "I did it for you."

Raz looked at me again, over his shoulder, then back at Maya. And the weirdest thing happened. Nothing.

He didn't know what to say. Maya was due a bollocking, but he was into her, wasn't he. Turned him all soft. He couldn't hit her. Couldn't knob her. Couldn't do fuck all.

"For you," she whispered. "For looking after me."

She stepped forward and touched his arm, gazing up at him. The two of them stood there. He gazed back.

He shook her off. Handed the phone to me.

"Get rid of this, la'," he said. "And search the whole house. Make sure there's no more knock-offs lying around."

He stomped out and shut himself in his room.

I looked at Maya. I tried to say something but she didn't wait to hear it. She gave me a crooked smile and went into the kitchen.

I waited on the roof at midnight. No sign of Maya. I sat there, smoking her skunk and thinking.

I could see why she owned up. Looking after herself, in a funny way. Made it seem like she cared for him. Made her seem a bit slow an' all. Loopy kind of gift, like a cat bringing you in a dead bird. He couldn't bollock her the way he could one of the lads. She'd got her claws in him. But he'd get his into her too.

He must be with her now, I thought. His nightly visit. Give her the meds. Her trying to find out his plans. Bit of pillow talk. Him holding out for more. Not getting it. At least I hoped not. But what did I know? I didn't know anything about Maya really. Never guessed she'd stick her neck out for me like that. No one made her do it. Why did she? Because she liked me? Or because she had plans of her own? It was true, what she'd said. There was a lot of things I didn't know.

She'd saved my arse with Raz, but it had put all kinds of thoughts in my head. The way she looked at him. Acting? I couldn't be sure. It gave me a nasty suss feeling that I couldn't shake.

I'd been sat there worrying a whole hour when I heard a noise behind me. At last. Her head popped through the skylight. I coughed my smoke out.

She slid softly down the tiles and sat cross-legged beside me. Snatched the spliff from my hand.

"You headcase," I said.

"You're welcome."

She took three huge drags, piling them up in her lungs.

I must have been getting too into her, because I felt like I was owed something. When she didn't speak, I felt miffed. After all that waiting, least she could do was talk to me.

"You've had a nice long bedtime story," I said.

"Lucky me."

She thrust the spliff against my chest. Spilt hot rocks in my lap. I grabbed it clumsily from her fingers. Saw them shaking.

I jumped up, patting and batting the sparks off my trackies. She lay back against the roof, trembling, slowly calming down. Alright, Azo, I thought. Back off. Done you a favour, hasn't she. Last thing she needs now is you winding her up.

I sat down again. She shifted closer to me. Her knee touched my leg. I put my hand down and squeezed it.

"So what did he say?" I asked her. "What did he do?"

She sighed and sparked up a Regal. "Nothing. Won't hardly talk. Just stares and mutters to himself."

"He still miffed about the phone?"

"Don't know. For that. Or because I'll not get off with him."

"I'll have a word."

"No," she said. "I'll handle him."

"Don't be soft."

"I'll handle him," she snapped.

I puffed on the spliff. "How? By hacking his mails?"

"For a start."

"Then what?"

She sighed.

"You don't know, do you?"

She stared at her lap. "Yes. I do," she said. Sounded like she was talking to a five-year-old kid.

I watched her. The gear had made my face go numb. My bottom lip was hanging down. I must have looked like a right gormless sod. She sighed again.

"I'll clean him out. His money."

The spliff was nearly dropping out of my fingers. She snatched it back.

"You know how to hack his bank?"

She sucked the spliff almost to the end.

"Not the bank. You hack the person. You stick spyware on them. Log all their passwords and secret shit. All the stuff they enter in web forms. Even the words they search for tell you stuff. Then you get in their online banking. Or if they're not using it, you get their numbers and passwords and you phone their bank yourself."

She ground the spliff out. I was too chonged to roll another. I took one of her Regals.

"So you're going to slip him a spy bug on his laptop?" I said.

"What do you think I was doing the other day?"

We looked out over the rooftops and the orange street lights.

How was I going to handle Maya? If she messed with Raz, it

119

would tip the house on his head. That wouldn't be good for anyone. Least of all me. I'd thought I'd ditch Paterson before I met her. But next to Maya, he was a safe pair of hands.

I wondered if I should trust her. Just weed fear, maybe. I tried to keep my spy head on. But I felt myself losing my rag, bit by bit.

"Why are you even here, if you're so sorted?" I said.

"Not that sorted. I've made enemies, haven't I. Need somewhere to shelter."

"Raz?" I snorted with laughter. "He's up to something. Not sure I'd call it giving us shelter. Why did you pick him?"

She looked at me and lit a Regal.

"The bank," she mumbled.

"Eh?"

"Where I worked."

"You told me it went tits up."

"I went out with one of the managers. Right gobshite. He let stuff slip. I hacked him. Got hold of some passwords."

"I know some boss cheats to Battlefield 4. Can I be in your gang?"

"Cheats? I already know them."

I shut up while she enjoyed that. Then she went on.

"This dickhead let me know when the bank was about to go down. I got out first. Took a bunch of data with me. Ripped off a load of card numbers. Printed new cards."

"You must be minted."

"My arse. I spend it as I go. Half of it I give to my mum."

"Why?"

"Pay off her house."

"Isn't that her job?"

"It's my fault. I sold her the loan. And she's sick. Needs this, needs that."

"Why did you come here then?"

"The list of bank accounts I nicked. Raz was on it."

I wanted to slap her arse and kiss her at the same time.

"You've already been in his bank files? You know where he gets his money?"

"Lots of funny places. Only now he's switched to some

other bank."

I frowned and swore to myself. This was all boss, but I couldn't do anything about it without Paterson. It might have been enough to get me out of there and back to Ali. Raz wouldn't even trace it to me. But that prick Paterson wasn't answering the Azo hotline. I didn't even know if he'd had my letter.

I clenched my teeth thinking of Paterson. Then I looked at Maya. Something about her still didn't add up.

"Why are you telling me all this?" I said. "I could grass you up."

"Nah," she said. "You're more the look-after-me kind."

"Don't take me for granted."

"Alright," she sighed. "I won't. You're a good lad, Azo. I had to tell you, cos I need your help."

"Oh yeah?"

"It's Raz."

"I told you, if he touches you, I'll have him."

"That wouldn't fix it."

"Why? What's the worst he can do?"

"He's done it already. I can clean Raz out. But I can't hack him if I'm not thinking straight."

I gritted my teeth. "What's he done?"

"He's punishing me for that phone. He's stopped giving me my pills."

Chapter Twenty-Five

On Saturday morning Raz and Mossie went out to meet some friends of theirs. They took Rodney with them. And Maya. I didn't like that. I knew what Rodney was thinking about me and her. Wondered what he might say. Most of all to Mossie. Wondered what Mossie would do if he stopped believing Maya was the good girl he'd hooked in the chatrooms.

I kept my mouth shut though. It wasn't the best time to be nagging, after that crap with Raz and the phone.

As they were leaving, Maya came into the hall. She had a dark blue headscarf on.

She didn't say anything. Mossie showed up behind her and helped her on with her coat. I told myself she knew what she was doing. When Mossie saw her, he had this smug look that I'd not seen on him before.

No teaching or training for the other lads today, Raz said. Day off. I stayed home with them and made them do the housework. Washing dishes, hanging clothes on the line. I got Hanzi scrubbing the bogs. He'd thank me for it one day. I thought I'd send the Manc down the garage for milk and bread, but I couldn't find him. His stuff was still in his room but his coat was gone from the hall.

I sat around, drinking tea and chewing my nails. Wondering if Paterson had got my letter.

They got back about teatime and Maya went straight to her room.

Come night I sat up on my bed with the skylight open, ready to climb up there when Maya came. She didn't.

I gave it an hour. Sat there wondering what Raz and Rodney got up to on their outing. They'd not told me anything. I smoked three Regals. Listened to the water pipes groaning. Then another noise, sharper than the others. A little clink and rattle.

I climbed down to the landing and stood at the banister to listen. Another rattle downstairs. Someone was undoing the chain on the front.

The porch door scraped.

I nipped back up to my room, put my trainies on, grabbed my trackie top off the bed and my house key from the bedside table. Then I crept back to the landing and downstairs.

The front door was standing open. To the right of it, light was coming from under Maya's door. Snores from behind Raz's across the hall. I pushed Maya's open and looked in. Her bedside lamp was on but the bed was empty.

I remembered what happened last time I went walkabout without telling Raz. Almost choked me, he did. God knew what he'd do if he caught me bunking off in the middle of the night.

I tiptoed past his room, stepped out the front door and clicked it gently shut behind me. Down the path and out the gate. I looked up and down the road then set off to the right. Then right again, towards the roundabout.

By the garage I glimpsed something white. Maya in just her vest, heading for the crossroads and the canal. No headscarf now. Barefoot, from the slow waddly way she moved. Hands down and out by her sides.

I started to run. Stopped. If I had a real heart in me, I'd catch her up, I thought. Put my arm round her. Take her straight back. But my heart was all twisted out of shape. I did what I was trained for instead. Sneaked along behind her and watched where she went.

She crossed the walkway over the canal and took the steps down to Church Road. Skirted the roundabout by the Lidl and dropped into the shadows under the railway bridge.

I jogged under there after her and turned into the foot tunnel leading up to the trains. There she was at the top of it, lit up by the yellow lights.

Midnight. The guards had gone home. I got up there as the last train was pulling in.

She was at the far end. She got in the back carriage.

I jumped in the front one as the doors hissed shut. Back on

the Northern Line, eh. Where all my troubles started.

It clattered off towards Crosby.

Hardly anyone in my carriage. A couple of smelly-rockers sat a few rows away, copping off with big tongues under a blinking tube light.

I stood by the doors with my hood up and watched the black mounds of the scrap yards speeding by.

When the train stopped, I pulled my hood down and popped my head out the doors to look back up the platform. Empty. The grey metal shelter, yellow bench. No one got on or off.

The doors squeezed shut again and it rolled on through Crosby. Big houses now. Leafy streets. Soon we were right out of the city, cutting through the dunes and golf links to Hightown. No one got off there either.

Over a level crossing, then a platform, shelters. Formby. It slowed down and jerked to a stop. Doors.

I stuck my head out.

There she was. Her white top under the yellow lights. By the back carriage, at the platform gate. She went through it, out of sight.

I ran after her, out onto the road. All hush. Trees. Big houses and cars. The gates had come back up to open the level crossing. Beyond it, there was the white top, heading east.

I followed her.

She hit a roundabout and turned left. I caught up two minutes later. A wide road lined with big gateposts.

No one about but us two. I trailed her as close as I could. Weren't many cars to hide behind. They were all parked up on these big gravel drives. I crept along in the shadow of the hedges instead, and tried to keep sight of Maya.

All hot and still, the night was. I heard her bare feet slapping on the tarmac. Her smoker's wheeze.

She crossed the road and stopped at the gate to one of the big houses. Big red-brick job. Blue flicker of a telly on the walls upstairs.

Maya reached in the pocket of her trackie bottoms and lit a ciggie. She stood there in the gateway, staring up at the house as she smoked. Then she tossed the fag away and crunched over the stones up the drive.

I was about to call out to her when a light went on in the house.

I crept across the road and up to the driveway. Hid behind the gatepost and peered round it at the upstairs window.

A woman was standing in it. A frizzy mop of hair backlit by the telly light. Maya stepped to the front porch and rang the bell, then backed off again onto the drive.

I crouched in the shadows and watched.

The woman vanished from the window and turned up a minute later down in the porch, rattling around with a key in the outer door. Maya's shoulders tightened.

The door scraped open on the stones and the woman stepped out under the porch light.

"Hiya," I heard Maya say, all soft and scared. She was blocking my view of the woman, but I heard the voice come in reply, husky and faint.

"Who's that?"

Maya sighed and fiddled with her fringe. "Me."

"Uh? Oh," the woman said.

She stepped towards Maya. Grey frizz of hair in the porch light. I craned my neck round the gatepost, my cheek against the brick, to get a better look at her. Heard Maya's reply.

"I need my pills."

"Oh. You not so well?"

I couldn't tell if she was mean, this one, or just slow.

"I've got none," Maya went on. "You know what'll happen." Her voice was breaking. She tugged her fringe like a little girl. "Please, mum."

I pulled myself back behind the gatepost. Pushed my forehead against it and bit my lip.

Maya was in tears. "I need them," she said again.

"Is that all?"

I caught Maya's reply through the sobs.

"Please. I'll look after you. I want to come back."

"I thought you just wanted the pills?"

Maya spluttered and snorted with tears.

"I'm sorry!" she said. "I miss you."

"Oh. Have you got any money?"

She sounded soft in the head. Maya didn't say anything.

"Are you working?"

"Course not," Maya said.

"Oh."

I peeped round the gatepost again. Maya had fallen to her knees. Her mum was lighting a fag. She looked down at Maya through the smoke, crunched two steps towards her and touched her head. Smoothed her hair. Pulled her gently to her feet. The fingers clasped her shoulder, then both the hands went to her back. Hugging.

Maya straightened up. The woman's face showed over her shoulder, the chin resting on it. I got a full view of her in the porch light.

She had the same stubborn gob as Maya. And something about the eyebrows. Arched upward. All bolshy and sad at the same time.

I stared too long. Careless. Sprang back out of sight behind the gatepost. Too late.

She'd seen me.

I heard a scuffling, scraping sound. When I looked again Maya was sitting on the gravel rubbing her elbow. Her mum reached down and grabbed her by the hair.

"After your pills, love?" she hissed. "Well who's that? One of your junkies come to rip the place off?"

Maya was on her knees, gripping her mum's wrist. Trying to free the fistful of hair. Whimpering. She twisted her head round and looked where her mum was pointing. At me. Anger spread on her face.

No point hiding now. I got up and stepped onto the drive.

"I just wanted to talk to you," I said.

Maya was looking at me like she'd rather I fucked off.

"Come 'ead," I said. "Leave her alone."

Her mum looked at her. "He's nice, this Paki," she said. "Where did you find him?"

Maya struggled to her feet. Wrenched the hand off her head, losing hair with it. She broke away towards me but her mum caught up.

126

"Where do you think you're going?" she yelled. She put her hands round Maya's neck from behind and pushed her to her knees. Grabbed her hair again and twisted her round to slap her.

I ran over and got between them. Held her mum's wrists and prised them off. Tried to trundle her back to the house. She swore. I locked her wrists down behind her back, shoved her into the porch and closed it.

I glanced up at the house next door. Lights coming on there. Window sliding open. Voices.

I turned back towards Maya.

The porch door rattled behind me. Opened. Maya's mum jumped on my back. I shook her off and whipped round. She came again, slapping at my face. I reached out and grabbed her shoulders. Held her off.

I got my fingers round her neck. That slowed her down.

Maya yelled at me to stop. Her mum went for my face again.

I thrust her to the ground but kept hold of her neck. Looked in her eyes and squeezed. One fist on top of the other. One-potato, two-potato. Wrung her like a dishcloth till she ran out of strength.

I heard Maya sobbing, further off than before. I turned round and she was gone from the drive. Gash of scattered stones where she'd gone down.

I eased my grip and left her mum wheezing on the gravel.

I ran to the gate.

Chapter Twenty-Six

Maya was a hundred yards off, legging flat out down the middle of the road. I caught her up. Tried to talk to her. She'd not look at me.

There was a noise. Flicker of blue pig car lights up ahead.

I put my arm round Maya and pulled her off to the left, through a little alley between two houses. She broke free of me and ran ahead.

I followed her down a cul-de-sac, another alley, and so on. Weaving around northwards, avoiding the bigger streets. Panting after her in the darkness.

We came out by another rail crossing. Another leafy road of big houses.

I stopped and caught my breath. Looked both ways and listened for cars. Heard the faint sound of one a street or two away. Maya had turned left and was running along the pavement, leaving red prints with her bleeding feet.

I called out but she'd not listen. I started running again. Keeping Maya in sight.

After twenty minutes the road got narrower, with wooden posts lining either side. The tarmac turned to sand and woodchips under my feet. Pines, towering overhead. No more lampposts. I kept running. The darkness calmed me. The salty sea smell.

Formby pine woods, eh. My mum took me there as a kid. Red squirrels, that was the big thing there. I remembered her pointing them out to me, these slinky little meffs running up and down the tree trunks. Gobbling nuts and poking their heads out the nesting boxes.

Endangered, they were. Too chinless to stay alive on their own. Give the grey squirrels a chance, they'd come and steal the red ones' nuts and shag their birds. So they had to live in this wood, the poncy reds, munching their pine nuts and not knowing how nasty life outside was.

My thoughts were racing. I slapped myself. Snap out of it, soft lad. Kept my eyes on Maya's white top up ahead. Listened to my own footsteps and breathing.

Not for long.

A whoop and a bleep. I spun round to look. Far behind me along the path, through the tunnel of pines, the blue lights of the bizzie car.

Keep going, Azo lad. But where? Hide in a tree? And Maya? What you going to do when you reach her? They'll only bring her in too when they catch you up.

Further on the forest thinned out and the path broadened into the sand dunes. Maya was still pelting along but the sand was slowing her down. I legged on after her, puffing up over the steep dunes and sliding down them.

I caught her up at last.

I put my arm round her shoulder. She shoved me off. I tried again. She swung her fist and cracked me on the jaw. I hardly felt it.

"I just want to talk to you," I said.

"You were going to kill her."

She hit me again. I put both arms round her and kissed her. My teeth scraped her cheek as she struggled. Her face was basted in tears and snot. She bit and scratched me but still I held on. We keeled over onto the sand, the pine needles and rabbit droppings.

I kissed her neck. I was crying too now. Hugging as if to make her feel better, but really it was me that needed that. I clung on like a scared kid.

She touched my lips with her fingers. My face. My hair. Trying to calm me down so she could prise my hands off.

I heard shouts through a loudhailer. Couldn't make out the words. Torches came flashing behind us on the forest path, moving closer. When I turned to look, Maya shoved me away. She struggled to her feet and ran off, scaling the next dune.

I scrambled after her, up and over and down. Another dozen feet, and there we were on the beach. Miles of flat wet sand and the Irish Sea.

Maya set off running again. She went quicker on the firm

sand, rustling through stacks of seaweed and crunching on razor shells. Running to the water.

All my strength had gone. A stitch in my side was killing me. My lungs were burnt out.

I couldn't run anymore.

Her white top faded out of sight in the dark.

I thought about running back to hide in the dunes. To burrow into one and let it fall in on top of me.

No time. There were the torches, flashing over the crests of sand. The slobbering and panting of the rozzer-dogs. And now the bizzies could see me. One was shouting at me to stand still.

I turned back to face the sea. Looked right, towards Southport. Left towards town. No sign of Maya.

The bizzies were yelling louder. I turned towards them. I heard another car behind me on the beach.

I span round.

Ragging along it was. Must be bizzies, I thought. But there was no blue flash. It braked a few yards away with a skid and a scatter of sand. The headlights shone on me. A door clicked open and a feller got out the back.

He stood there in the beams.

I lifted a hand again to shield my eyes. Tried to get a look at him. All I could see was his dark suit.

He held the car door open.

"Jump in." he said.

I glanced over my shoulder at the torches coming down the dunes. Then I was in the back of the car, watching through the tinted window as the bizzies hit the beach with their torches.

Paterson got in next to me and the car started crawling. A blacked-out screen blocked my view of the driver.

He patted my knee. I flinched.

"Well," he said. All fake and chirpy. "I thought we'd have a talk. The three of us."

"Eh?"

"Let's pick up your girlfriend. Maya, isn't it?"

"Leave her alone. She's nothing to do with it."

He frowned and pouted.

"She's not!" I told him. Wondered if I could do something

right for Maya at last. Spare her having to meet that twat.

"I've not told her nothing," I said. "We've just been copping off."

He laughed, staring out the window. His eyes scanning the sand.

"You've got a good heart, Azo," he said. "Shame about that."

He tapped on the glass behind the driver. The car stopped with a jolt. Paterson jumped out and strode off.

A minute later he was back, pushing Maya in first. She sat in the middle, between me and him. He pulled the door to. I felt the locks clunk home all round us. Paterson smoothed his fringe back.

"Don't worry, Maya," he said. "I'll have you back home soon. Raz'll never know you were gone."

She stared at him.

"Let her go," I said. "I told you. She's nothing to do with all this."

"You could have fooled me, Azo. Chasing her in the moonlight? She must be someone special," he said. Sarky bastard. "But what do I know? I'm catching up."

"You weren't taking my calls. Why don't we start with that?"

Maya turned and looked at me, wondering what I'd got her into. Wondering who I was.

I'd messed things up for her tonight alright. I'd do what I could to make up for it. Best I could do now was get Paterson to look after her. Rescue her from Raz and Mossie and whoever the scums were who she'd worn the headscarf for. Get her safe and then hunker back down in the house. Get on with the job by myself.

"Look," I said. "Do what you want to me. I'll take the rap for that lad at The Grace. But you've got to help her. Don't make her go back to Raz."

"Why ever not?"

"He's got plans for her. God knows what. Sick shit. She's not safe."

He raised his eyebrows like a smartarse.

"She's no use to you," I told him.

Paterson shifted in his seat and twisted round to face Maya. "Oh, but she is though," he said. He smiled at her. "Hello. Paterson."

He held his hand out. She didn't shake it.

He tapped on the tinted glass in front of him. The car started moving again, along the sand towards the city with the sea to our right.

Paterson looked at Maya.

"There's something Azo's not told you, love," he said.

She glanced at me, her cheeks splatched with tears. Then she turned her face away.

"Azo's not just some scally working for Raz," Paterson went on. "He works for me too."

"And who are you then, granddad?" she snapped.

Paterson twisted round further in his seat. He grabbed her hand and moved his face close to hers. She squirmed. He gripped her tighter.

"Why's a nice girl like you hanging around with Raz?"

She shrugged. He went on. "You need him to look after you, don't you Maya? You're on the run. It was naughty what you did at the bank."

He let it sink in, watching her face right close up.

She sniffed. "So you're a bizzie."

Paterson sighed. He stared past her out of the window like he wasn't listening and scratched his head.

"Poor Maya," he said. "Always the same drill. You get out of your depth. You run away. Run out of pills. Hit a downer. You can't win. You should have been on holiday this summer. Instead you're living with Raz and Mossie. Getting back to your roots? Or are you up to more naughtiness?"

"How do you…"

He tapped his head. "I've got a file on you, love."

Maya spoke again, softer this time.

"The bank," she said. "I'll tell you who else ripped it off."

Paterson laughed, throwing his head back and showing all his teeth.

"I already know that, Maya. But thanks. It's sweet of you.

Next time I want some insider tips, I'll know who to call."

Her face had gone pale. Her voice came out all soft. "I thought that was what you nicked me for," she said.

"Maya, Maya," Paterson said, patting her on the knee. "You're not nicked. I'd have to fill out all *kinds* of paperwork. I picked you up so you can help me. You're on the inside there with Raz. Even closer to him than Azo is. And not only him. Mossie. Rodney. And the leaders of the meetings in Warrington. You're close to where the money is. That's where we want to be. Where Azo could never quite reach."

She blinked. "If you're not nicking us, stick it up your arse. I'll not go back to Raz now."

Paterson shook his head gently. His face hardened.

"Maya," he said. "Your mum's lying there on her driveway, turning stiff. Who are we going to blame for that?"

She stared at him. No words. She stared at me.

"No she's not," I said. "I let go of her. Go back and see."

Her eyes filled with tears. Paterson watched them brim up and scatter.

"She was breathing when I run off," I said.

"Well I dropped by to see her straight after," Paterson said. "She's not breathing now."

Maya shut her eyes as she cried.

"Any ideas?" Paterson said. "Who can we blame?"

Her face crinkled. Forehead, nose, cheeks. She bowed her head and lurched into big heaving sobs.

"Who do you think?" she spat.

"You don't mean Azo?" he said. "He wasn't there."

She raised her head, her face sticky with tears, her fringe matted with sweat and sand.

"Azo's not been anywhere for months," Paterson said. "He works for me, Maya. Off the grid. So will you be, if you join in. Off it for good. You'll be safe. If I turn you loose here and now, you'll be caught in no time."

"Fuck off," she whispered. She flopped her head down, sobs jerking at her neck.

I wanted to reach over and touch her. But Paterson sniffed and banged the last nail in.

"Why would you do it, I wonder? Perhaps she threatened to turn you in. Anyway. Murder on top of fraud. That'll get you life."

Maya had gone still. I started thinking she'd passed out. Then she coughed.

"What'll it be, love?" he asked her. "Go down, or work for me? I'll sort out your pills."

Nothing.

"You're a good girl," he told her. "You act tough, but you're kind inside. You want a quiet life, don't you? Well I can help you have that." He patted her knee. "Good girl."

He changed his tone. Business.

"Raz is going to be moving those lads around," he said. "He may be moving you too. I want to know where. Azo knows how to reach me."

He dropped Maya off back at the roundabout, out of sight of the house. I gave her my key and asked her to leave the latch up. She took it without a word. Wouldn't meet my eye.

After she was out, Paterson pulled the door to. The car moved off again, crawling round the block.

"Nice girl," Paterson said.

"She doesn't know what she's doing," I said. "She's sick."

"Bipolar. I've seen worse."

"And now you've killed her mum?"

He didn't answer. "Maya will be alright."

He reached in his pocket and handed me this little paper bag.

"For Maya. Lithium, valproate, olanzapine. I've written the dosing on the box. To you, for safekeeping."

I'd been waiting for him to nab me. Now here he was, and not a word about what I'd done. What was worse than him pulling me out of the game? Keeping me in it, and dragging Maya in too.

"So," he said. "I was in your neck of the woods a few weeks back. They were peeling someone off the tracks. The friend of the lad you ran into in The Grace."

"You said you'd always be on the end of the line for me," I yelled at him. "Any time. Help me out, like I was helping you. Where were you that night?"

He looked down at his lap and let out a big sigh.

"Alright, Azo. I'll come clean. I was letting you stew."

"I'm dead if Raz finds out who I am. And you're the one sulking?"

He turned his head and looked me hard in the eye.

"We saw you. You went to meet your boy."

I wanted to hit him. I twitched. Breathed. Stopped myself. Thought for a sec. I reached in my pocket, grabbed the Nokia and stuck it in his lap. He looked down at it, cleared his throat and picked it up.

"Hold on to this, Azo. You'll be needing it."

He tried to stuff it back in my trackie. I wriggled but he rammed his hand down, leaving the Nokia in my pocket. He straightened up in his seat.

"You made it very hard for me, you know," he said. "Going to see little Ali like that. By the rules, I should have hauled you in."

"Then why didn't you?"

"This job you're on. I could feel it was a big one. Now it's heating up. Thanks for your letter by the way. So Raz had you picking up his mail at Tranmere. Guns from the Balkans?"

I looked down at my lap. "No. The guns came in a container through Bootle. At Tranmere it was this case. Kind of safe box. And he's got a fridge that's locked. I reckon he's put the box in there."

Paterson froze. Just for the shortest sec. He nearly looked worried.

"The ship came from Liberia," he said. "That's what Raz said."

He nodded.

"You know more about all this than I do."

"Not enough," Paterson said. "I've got to keep my hooks in Raz. I couldn't cut you loose. I bent the rules for you. Even though you did let me down. I wanted to see if you'd hang in there without me. If you'd wanted to bail you were smart enough to do it without my help. But if you sat tight you were my kind of man. That was the test, Azo. You passed."

He had the driver head to Litherland.

"Remember what I told your girlfriend," Paterson said. "The lads are going to start moving around soon. Find out who handles them. Raz's friends. The links in the chain."

"Moving around? Why?"

"You tell me. Work together. See where they go. And don't lose sight of Raz."

"He's waiting for me to slip up so he can do me."

He reached over and grabbed my shirt in his fist. He tugged me towards him. Pulled my face right close to his. I smelt cough syrup on his breath and apple shampoo in his hair.

"You do what you've got to do," he whispered. "You keep in with him, lad, do you hear?"

I nodded.

"And you get inside that fridge."

We were back at the roundabout in Litherland.

"When will you let me see my boy?" I asked him. Broken record.

"When Raz and all his friends are banged up," Paterson said.

"You're a fanny flap."

"And you are a bard and a gentleman."

I climbed out. Paterson called out to me as I was walking off.

"I'll be answering the phone from now on," he said.

She'd left the front door open. I slipped inside, clicked the latch gently behind me and stood there, listening. To my right came snores from Raz's bedroom. I looked left at Maya's door. No light from under it. I pushed it open a crack and stuck my head round.

In the glow from a streetlight, I could make out the shape of her, lying in bed on her side. I stepped forward and peered close at her face. Her eyes were open, staring at the wall.

I sat down beside her on the bed.

She didn't move.

I took Paterson's paper bag out my pocket, opened one of the boxes from it and split out a pill. Put my fingers to her mouth and worked it between her lips.

She moaned, gurgled and tried to swallow. I put Paterson's

bottle of water in her hands and wrapped her fingers round it. Unscrewed the top and put the bottle to her lips. Poured some in her mouth. She coughed and water slopped down the pillow.

I thought about leaving her with the rest of the pack. Thought again. I put the pills back in my trackie pocket. Went to the door and turned.

Her   eyes   had   closed.

Chapter Twenty-Seven

I looked at the Nokia. Nine a.m. I crawled out of bed, limbs aching. I limped downstairs.

The lads were getting dressed and having their showers. No sign of Raz. No Rodney. Still no Manc. I looked in Maya's room. Her bed was empty. I kept the pills in my pocket for when I saw her.

I went in the kitchen and got the bowls and cereals out for breakfast. When the lads had all come down, I left Casho in charge and said I'd go to the garage myself for the shopping. As I was taking my coat off the banister I stopped and looked at the space next to it. That cellar door. I'd hardly looked twice at it since I'd been here.

Just a Yale lock like the one on Raz's door. I'd have to see about that. Have to get another look at the fridge too. Have another crack at picking the locks. For that I'd have to get hold of the Manc.

Raz showed up about six with the other three. Maya in her headscarf, pale and quiet. Rodney was all smug. Like there was something big going on and it was all about him.

I asked Raz where they'd been. He patted me on the shoulder.

"Tomorrow you drive me," he said. "I tell you all about it."

"Tell me now," I said.

He gave me this look, then melted into his old mad grin and whacked me on the shoulder. Rodney smirked to himself.

Raz told Casho and Ayax to take care of dinner and sent Maya to her room. She popped to the bog first. I left pills by her bedside with water for her to find when she came down.

She came out of her room later to eat with us. Worn out. Pale. She wouldn't look me in the eye.

When he'd finished eating, Raz threw down his napkin and slapped his belly. He stood up, scraping his chair back on the floor. He snapped his fingers and pointed at Maya, then jerked his thumb sideways towards her room.

"Little Bo-Peep. Go to sleep," he said.

She slunk off.

"Too much work makes Jill a sleepy bunny," Raz said.

He snapped his fingers again, at Hanzi this time. Pointed to the sink. Casho had stacked our dishes there. Hanzi started washing up.

Raz stretched his arms. He leaned over and slapped my shoulder.

"Come 'ead, Azo, la'," he said. "To work."

He led me out of the kitchen. Rodney followed. He'd been quiet all tea. Or his mouth had at least. That hum of smug-arseness off him had got a notch or two louder since he'd been popping out on trips with the two big men.

I glanced back as Raz led us into the hall. I caught Rodney's eye. This nasty smirk on his gob.

Raz had stopped by the cellar door. Key in his hand.

"You told us it was jammed."

He unlocked it and opened the door.

"Something you need to see, la'."

He pointed down the steps. A dim glow came from the bottom.

I used to think of my dad when I was scared. I'd never known whether he was brave or good or anything. That's what had given him his power. He was so deep and dark and unknown. Like that song in infants they used to sing about God. So high you can't get over it, so wide you can't get round it. Wonderful love. It gave me strength, that deepness. He was like God, my dad. He could be anything I made him.

He wasn't there though now, was he. He'd not save me from Raz. And Raz had it in for me. I could tell that now. I wasn't meant to walk out of this cellar. I felt it in my gut, my heart, my head. I started hearing words. No clue where they came from. They told me this was it.

I took hold of the dusty hand rail and put my foot on the top step. My legs were trembling. I started hobbling down the stone staircase into the gloom. Raz and Rodney clumping down behind me.

I thought of Ali. I wondered what he was doing. Having his bath. Playing with his Buzz Lightyear. He'd be starting school soon. Did he ask for me? Did he think of me when I wasn't there? How long had it been? Three months? Like a lifetime for a lad that young. All that life I'd missed. All them weekends wasted. Every day taking me further from him.

There were stacks of wooden crates all over the floor at the bottom. A big torch lying on its side, switched on.

Raz stood in the glare of the torch, his legs planted wide and arms folded. Rodney sat down on the bottom step.

Raz frowned. "We've been worried about you," he said.

"Eh?"

"You're not yourself, Azo. Something bugging you. Wondering what."

"I'm knackered, aren't I? Looking after five lads."

He reached in the pocket of his combat shorts and lit up a Regal.

"So where'd you take Rodney today?" I said.

"Not sure I can tell you, la'."

"What's the matter? Am I not in the gang anymore?"

"I don't know," he said. "Are you?"

"Get lost."

I turned my back on him and sparked up a ciggie of my own.

Raz came after me and grabbed my arm. Grip like wire-cutters. He pulled me back round to face him.

"Where'd you sneak out to last night?" he said. "I heard you coming back in."

I sighed. "I was seeing that bird I told you about."

"Oh ay, yeah. Knobbed her yet?"

"No, I haven't."

"That's taking a while. She Catholic?"

"Fuck off."

He shrugged. Then he went and flicked a switch at the bottom of the stairs. A bulb lit up at the far end of the cellar. It was hanging from the ceiling behind a chest-high line of crates. Three-yard gap on the other side there was, between the stack and the wall. Raz plodded over there, stepped into the gap and beckoned to me.

There was something round there. Raz was looking at it, smiling. He beckoned me on again. I stepped round the stack in front him and looked.

Wooden chair. No one was sitting in it. He was on the bare floor instead. Lying there, in white boxies, blood and drool.

Manc Lee.

He wasn't moving. He looked hardly alive. Blood was crusted round his nose and lips and hair pasted to his head. One eye swollen shut. Wrists together behind his back in old chain handcuffs.

Rodney stooped down and grabbed him. He yanked him up and planted him backwards in the chair.

The Manc sat slumped with his head lolling to the right. He squinted with his less bad eye and saw me standing there. Then he saw Raz and shuddered.

"Fuckin' hell, Raz," I said.

Raz stepped towards the chair. The Manc twitched and jerked. He scraped the legs an inch backwards and came to rest, breathing all heavy and snotty through his nose.

"Raz," I said. "What have you done?"

Raz leaned closer to him. More jerking and scraping. The Manc was backed up against the wall now.

"No, la'. Ask him what *he*'s done."

I looked at the Manc. He didn't look up to talking.

I turned to Raz. He turned to Rodney.

"I caught him with this," Rodney said.

He reached round behind him as he spoke and pulled something from the belt of his jeans. He held it out under the hanging bulb so I could see. A black Sig.

Rodney held it like a pro, with his finger stretched out safely along the barrel, not curled ready around the trigger like a jumpy scally. He gave us this hard frown.

I knew what had happened but I didn't let on. I made a fake sigh like I couldn't believe it. "So he's got a gun. Since when's that a shit-kicking crime?"

Raz let Rodney answer again. Even with my nerves like they were, the sound of his fake Windie scally twang made me want to slap him.

"He nicked it from us," Rodney said. "Ain't the only thing he nicked. He went in Raz's fridge."

He turned and glared down at the Manc. "Eh, you?" he said. "That wasn't very nice, was it?"

"Hang on," I said. "His fridge?"

"Where I keep my doctor's knick-knacks," Raz said. He grinned and his eyes glinted. "He thought he were nicking drugs. He were nicking something much worse than that. Could have killed us all."

The Manc had his gooey eyes fixed on me.

I turned to Raz again. "Hang on," I said. I wasn't sure how to finish that line. "You should look after him," I said. "He can help us out."

Raz frowned at me like I was off my head.

"I mean… He made a mistake, Raz, mate," I went on. "He got scared. He never meant to screw you over."

Raz frowned darker.

"Hey," said Rodney. "You knew about this?"

"No. It's just…" *I know this lad*, I wanted to say. *He's alright.* Same soppy crap you'd say for any mate. Couldn't though, could I. I'd made up my mind to stay in this game. For Ali's sake. For Maya's. I couldn't stick up for the Manc if Raz had him down as a back-stabber. I'd be no use to anyone sitting where the Manc was.

Rodney went on. "Little Hanzi tipped us off. I looked in on this gyppo in bed. He had this under the cover. He were holding onto it like his cock. Had the test tube under his pillow."

Raz had heard enough. He stepped round behind the chair and took something from his pocket. He bent down behind the Manc. Click. Stepped away with the cuffs in his hand.

The Manc's arms fell limp by his sides.

"Nice one, Raz," I said. "We all work together, eh?"

"Dead right, la'."

He reached behind him and took something from his own belt. Another of the Sig Sauer semis I'd seen in his box that day.

He turned to face the Manc.

Well I couldn't stop Raz, could I. Not if I wanted to walk out of there. Paterson would understand that.

Raz cocked the gun. I tried to swallow. Couldn't.

He took hold of the barrel and handed it to me.

"Here you go, la'," he said. "Show us whose side you're on."

I heard Rodney shuffling his feet behind me. Then a snap and a hiss as he blew a bubble with chewing gum and popped it. I looked at the Manc's mashed-up face.

The gun was heavier in my hand than the day before. Raz had loaded it. So he did have ammo. Another box to tick for Paterson there. Paterson. That twat. What was he'd said to me? *Do what you have to do, lad. Anything. I'll keep you safe.*

I smelt fag smoke from somewhere. I tried to think.

Eleven rounds there'd be in this gun in my hand, if it was full. Eleven in the one in Rodney's hand. I wasn't sure how handy he was. I could have him in a fight but there was a lot of things I was starting to wonder about Rodney. Then who knew what other bits and bobs Raz had on him. I didn't fancy my chances of making it out the door alive.

The Manc was eyeballing me through his good socket. I looked at him and slid my finger over the trigger. He spoke to me softly.

"Come off it, Azo," he said. "He'll do you next."

"Shush."

"Who you gonna betray next, Azo?" the Manc said. "Where does it end?"

Good point, that. I didn't know the answer. What I was doing? Whatever Raz told me, that's what. So much for all my training. All Paterson's arse-kissing about me being a great asset. I was a tool, like everyone in that house.

I muttered a prayer to myself as I stooped over the Manc. Not sure who I was talking to. I heard a bird fluttering its wings in my head. I muttered and whispered to myself faster and lighter.

I prodded the muzzle in the Manc's forehead and pulled the trigger twice.

Raz took the gun from my hand. I turned and looked at him.

His leery saggy lip. Then something caught my eye further behind me. A white top. Vest.

I hadn't seen Maya come in. She was standing there with her back against the stone wall, holding a fag to her mouth. She was looking at me. I couldn't tell if she was seeing me or not.

Raz slapped me on the back.

"Welcome back, la'," he said.

Chapter Twenty-Eight

Raz and Rodney carried him out in the night while I cleaned up the cellar. I keeled over into bed about three and dreamt of his mashed face and popped head. That wiped out the face of the lad on the tracks for a bit.

The two of them were still gone the next morning. I checked upstairs. Rodney had taken his clothes and his bag from his room.

Sunday. Meant to be my Ali day. Not this time.

As I got back downstairs I heard a key turning in the hall. A shape loomed through the frosted glass of the front door. Raz came in and slammed it behind him.

"Where's Rodney?" I said.

He didn't answer. Handed me the car keys.

"What about the lads?"

"They be alright. Casho and Ayax, they big enough."

I gripped the keys in my hand. He slapped my shoulder. "Come 'ead," he said.

He had me drive around a bit. Didn't speak. He looked at me from time to time and sat there thinking as I drove. We went down Princess Way and up the dock road to the Marina then on into Crosby till we got to the beach.

We parked up. Clear summer day. To the right, miles of grey water and slimy sand. A few miles along was the spot where Paterson picked me up two nights before. Crests of green grass on the tips of the dunes. Left, the docks. Containers and cranes and windmills. Further away, the hills of Wales in the haze. Nice it was, to see so far. Spy other places and wonder what was going on there. Made me feel part of some wider world.

We sat there in the Astra, staring at the sea a hundred yards off. All I could think about was the Manc.

"Did I pass the test then?" I said. I let a narky tone creep into my voice. "Or am I next?"

He lit up a ciggie. Then he spoke at last, staring out over the wet sand.

"You told me you had nothing, when I met you," he said. "Why did you not tell me you had a little boy?"

I couldn't move.

"Ali, isn't it?"

So that was it. Who'd told him? Maya? Or had he sent one of the lads to follow me one Sunday?

He made me tell him all about Ali and Leanne. The whole thing. How I felt about it. How I got friends with her at the ring, that summer after I left school. How fit and tough and smart she was. Boxing after work. Her good heart. Cared about me. Let me gob to her all about my dad. Daft friendship, me and this bird ten years older. Then that Friday night in the gym car park when she came out all dressed up for the night. Necking cider out of my bottle. Dragging me along to the Krazy House with her mate. Bar. Dancefloor. Taxi. Hers.

Then Ali.

Raz sat there in the car next to me, nodding at his lap.

"He's a good lad, eh?"

"Yeah."

"How old?"

"Four now."

He tossed his ciggie out of the window. "Hard for you."

I didn't answer. I sparked up one of my own. The smoke filled the space between us.

"Alright," I said. "You sussed. I been going to see him on my Sundays off. After his swimming class."

I looked up at him, all frightened orphan like. The same act I did to get hired by him. Go 'ead. Giz an Oscar.

"Don't kick me out, Raz mate. I'll do what you tell me. I've nowhere to go."

Raz rubbed his stubbly head and banged a fist on the dashboard.

"I done good work for you," I said. "Never crossed you. Never dissed you. Never let you down."

I wiped my eyes and sucked on my fag.

Raz sat there staring at the fuel gauge, then lifted his eyes and gazed out to sea. His mind was somewhere else. Lips moving, nodding, like he was chatting to someone in his head.

He turned to me.

"You're a good lad," he said. "Daft. Lost. But good. You did good last night. You'll do good for me again."

I sniffed and nodded.

"Must miss your boy?"

"Yeah," I said.

"Bring him to live with us."

I shuddered inside. A big icy broom handle right up my arse to the chest. So that was where my acting got me. I wasn't patting myself on the back anymore.

I smiled at him and snorted, like he couldn't mean it. I shook my head.

"Not allowed," I said. "He's with his mum."

"So?" Raz tapped the dashboard. "We go and get him."

"But she's…. there's…"

His turn to shrug. "Come 'ead," he said. Like there was nothing simpler in the world.

"They'll lock me up. Then I'll never get to see him."

"They never know where he is, la'! He be in the house of lads."

He patted my shoulder.

"How can he... What are we going to do with him?"

I wished I hadn't asked.

"He learn from me, la'. No mum. No welfare. None of them bell-ends. I teach him the way." Raz stopped and thought for a sec. "He can have Rodney's room," he said, and grinned. "Sunday today. Swimming class, right?"

I'd not seen it before. I'd thought Raz was just clever and hard. I saw it now though. He may have been both of those things, but he was fucking mad too.

If I dug my heels in he'd stop trusting me again.

There was only one way out. I'd kill him. Crash that lemon with the two of us in it. Sooner that than let him near Ali.

"Alright, Raz," I said. Playing it up again. Hopeless. Grateful. "Nice one."

I turned the key, palmed the Astra round in a circle and crunched back up to the give-way.

Raz was all daft and happy now, like some kid going to Disneyland. He wouldn't stop talking. I let him gas on. I was trying to work out how to get away and call Paterson. But I pricked my ears up when he talked about Rodney.

"I drove him to Speke this morning," Raz said.

"How come?"

Raz chuckled. "Catch the plane, la'. Above us only sky!"

"Eh? He going on holiday?"

I turned my head and saw him smirk at that. Calm, he was. I was back in the gang.

"More like a work trip," he said.

"Business class?"

"Right on, la'. There's poor fuckers pouring into this country, la'. Pay their life savings to wriggle through in the back of some lorry. Rodney though, he go the other way!"

Here was something Paterson could get his teeth into. I kept my eyes on the road and tried not to look too keen.

"So where's he going?" I said.

"Now you're askin', la'. Them poor fugees. Where d'you reckon they come from?"

"Don't know. Shitholes and wars."

He chuckled again. "Shitholes is right. Wars is right!"

And he went on. Told me the whole plan. Cheap flights. Liverpool to Madrid. Madrid to Istanbul. Then a big long ride to the Syrian border. All the way to that shitstorm you see on the news.

"My Albanians have got him a clean passport," Raz said. "Radars'll never bleep!"

"And when he gets there?"

Raz winked at me.

"Study trip," he said.

He leant over and gripped my shoulder. The burning sweat off his palm seeped through my shirt.

He made me stop on the main road in Crosby and got out. He crossed over and went into a fried chicken place.

I fumbled the Nokia out of my pocket. My hands were shaking. I dropped it. Picked it up. I stared across the road at Raz through the shop front, waiting in line for his chicken with his back to the road.

I slumped down in the seat and put the phone to my ear. It started ringing.

"Hello, lad."

All chilled out, Paterson sounded. I pictured him sitting there at Sunday lunch, passing the mushrooms to the vicar and wiping gravy off his chin.

I kept an eye on the chicken queue. Raz was nearly at the till. I sank further down in my seat.

"Listen. You've got to send some rozzers to the baths. Raz is going to snatch my boy."

"Raz?"

"He's found out about Ali," I tell him. "He wants him with us. He's sending Rodney off today for some jihadi crap in Syria."

"And the other lads too?"

"I guess so, sooner or later."

"Good work."

"You going to help me out then?"

"We can't go near Raz yet. That'd give the game away."

"I don't care about Raz. I'm talking about Ali."

"We can't just snatch him from his mother."

"Then there's going to be a car crash in Crosby. I'm not driving this mad twat to my little boy."

"Now then... "

"You'll be peeling me out of the wreck."

"Alright, Azo," he said. "Hear me out."

"Quick."

"Your friend Frank will be with him. He'll head Raz off."

"You lazy shit. You're leaving Frank to sort this out?"

"Azo, I can't snatch Raz now. We still haven't joined the dots. But we'll have Rodney when he tries to leave. Where's he flying from? Liverpool? Manchester? What name's he travelling under?"

"I'll tell you once you've rescued my kid."

"Now listen... "

"You nick Raz. Then you let me see Ali. Or you'll get no more out of me."

"Hold on, Azo. We've got to keep Raz out there and you with him. Until we know what he's up to and who with. That's how you'll get your boy."

"I'm crashing."

"Hold on!"

I stopped and listened.

"You're a good lad, Azo… "

"Stop. I might come in your mouth."

"I mean it. You're a good agent and I need you. I'm saying alright. You keep online with Raz and we'll see what we can do to let you spend some time with Ali. I'll get you some help."

"Rodney's flying from Speke to Madrid this morning."

I hung up and pocketed the phone. I turned the key as Raz got back in the car.

We passed through Litherland near the house, but he made me drive right on without stopping. Bootle, Walton. Down and down. South and east.

I started praying in my head. Don't let him get his hands on Ali. Nice one, Mr God mate. All this crap could be nearly over. If I could just get Raz nicked. I'd give Paterson everything. Mossie, Rodney. Even Casho and Ayax, the poor bastards. Little Hanzi? He'd be better off with Paterson. Wouldn't he? I'd help him stitch up the lot of them. Then I'd grab Ali, and Maya, and run.

Chapter Twenty-Nine

It was ten to eleven when we got to the baths. Ali's class would finish on the hour. Raz had me pull into the pool car park. He licked the chicken grease off his fingers.

"Alright, la'," he said. "When we see the kid, you go get him. I leave the Astra here with the engine running."

"You what? You bailing?"

"Have to keep my head down, me, la'. Got a lot of plates spinning."

The sly twat. Course he did. He wasn't that mad. He'd see how far I could go. Then he'd let them pin it on me. He'd be on a plane to the Middle East.

We sat there, not speaking. Twenty-five minutes. Then the pool door opened and kids started coming out.

Two more minutes. Three. Then there they were. Frank in his cap. Ali with wet hair, a bag of Nik Naks in one hand, orange armbands in the other hand. He was always running off with them. Frank hadn't spotted it. He could be a handful, little Ali.

"Who's this?" said Raz.

"It's Frank. I can handle him."

"Off you go, then."

He sunk down in his seat. I got out the car and looked around me. Spotted three bizzies across the street. Two fellers and a young woman, listening to her walkie-talkie. Raz couldn't see them from where he was sitting.

I walked over to the path near the gate.

"Alright Frank, mate."

"Leanne's inside," he said.

"I'd best be quick then."

I grabbed Ali, hugged and kissed him.

"How are you, lad?" I said.

"Crap!" he said, beaming at me. "Where you been?"

I turned back to Frank.

"Do me a favour?"

Frank lit a Benson. "She'll be out in a sec."

"Need my favour quick then."

He ruffled Ali's hair and pinched his cheek. Looked me in the eye.

"You're the boss."

"Hit me," I said.

"You kinky sod."

"Then this big bloke in the car's going to come at you. You're going to hit him an' all."

"There's a crew of bizzies across the road."

"Good."

He scratched his head and smoothed his hand over it. That daft way he did, like he still had hair.

"It's almost over, Frank. I need your help to finish it."

He looked at his fist and flexed it.

He was ready. No quezzies asked.

Frank bent down to Ali and put his arm round him. Told him to go inside and give the armbands back to Mrs Rimmer. Ali ran whooping and whistling through the swing-doors.

I glanced back at the car. Raz had watched Ali go. I saw his lips moving as he swore and punched the dashboard.

Frank put his right hand round the back of my head and leaned in like he was whispering in my ear. He dropped his hand to my shoulder and straightened his arm again, pushing me away. Cracked me on the jaw with his left.

Wicked hook it was. Wind and lightening. Spun me right round before I hit the paving.

I lay there for ten seconds before I could peel my head up off the ground.

Raz held back a bit. He must have been thrown by that. Then at last he was out of the Astra, striding across the car park in his shorts and para boots.

Frank didn't budge. He clicked his shoulders back, rolling and slackening them. Watching Raz come.

I should have been out cold after that punch, but the dreno cut through it. I rolled over. Crossed the paving and the grass on my hands and knees and scrambled to my feet. Bashed through the swing doors into the building.

I met Ali coming back from the poolside. Bent down and kissed him.

"Hold my hand, lad," I told him. To keep myself steady, as much as anything.

He put his hand in mine. Great it felt. He put his face to my thigh, hugging my legs. I covered the silky ball of his head with my palm. I stood by the door, looking out through the glass at Frank and Raz.

Raz was on the ground, Frank on top of him. Raz thrashing about. He couldn't struggle free. The bizzies were running across the road.

The policewoman came through the front gate. She looked at Raz and Frank as they got hustled to the pig cars. Then she looked towards the swinging doors, right at me.

I picked up Ali in my arms. God, he'd got heavy. I'd used to hold him by linking my hands under his bum. Now he slipped down. I hoiked him up high as I could, squeezed my arms round his chest, and ran.

Past the slots. Cash desk, toilets, changing rooms. Through to the poolside. They were stashing the armbands and hauling in the floating lane markers. Ali was staring at me up close with big eyes. Wondering what on earth his dad was up to.

I looked all round me. To my right, this bunch of mums picking up their bags and floats. Ali twisted round in my arms, shouted and waved. And there she was, right in the middle of them. Leanne.

I looked back through the glass of the poolside doors. Saw the rozzer in her yellow vest, getting closer.

I put Ali down and he ran to his mum. She lifted him and held him against her, kissing his cheek. Tired, she looked. Her arms had got stockier in the six months since I'd seen her. Her neck had got thicker and started gobbling up her chin. No sign of that cocky bird I'd known at the ring.

I thought of how she'd farted me about that last Sunday evening I saw her. Hadn't told me where Frank was. So I'd ended up at The Grace.

She stared at me and opened her mouth to speak. The doors

swished open behind me. The bizzie's walkie-talkie crackled.

I wondered how long it'd be before I'd get to see Ali again. Hours? If Raz went down and Paterson kept his word.

"Dad!" Ali shouted.

I looked at him there, hugged against his mum's waist. His red trainies. Black trackies riding up his legs. Beautiful little smile on him. His stumpy front teeth and glossy black mop. The shape of his face had changed. His nose had got bigger and flat at the top like mine.

"Dad!" He thought I was staying. Thought I was playing a game. "Dad! We gonnew 'ave beans?"

I bit my lip. Couldn't speak. Couldn't bear to look at him too long.

The bizzie yelled at me, but she was too late. Down the poolside there was a fire door. I pushed the bar and legged out into the car park.

A fleet of bizzies had boxed the Astra in.

I couldn't feel my jaw. Good old fear and dreno, drowning the pain, driving me on.

I fixed my eyes on the side wall of the car park. Ten feet high. Took a running leap and scrambled up it. The bizzie slammed out through the fire door and came yelling after me. I stood on the wall and looked at her. Dropped down the other side and pelted off through the jiggers.

Chapter Thirty

Maya was gone. Her room was the same mess as before. Raz's was locked like always. And the cellar. I went to the kitchen, took a pint glass out of the cupboard, filled it from the tap and glugged the lot down. I went up to check the other rooms.

The lads were all gone. Their bags and coats too.

I thought about Rodney. Would the other lads be headed that way too? They'd have missed the afternoon flight to Spain by now. They'd be going another way. Manchester? All sorts of flights from there. They could fly straight to Turkey.

Maya too? How long would her pills last? She'd never make it. They'd be burying her in the desert in a month.

I could call Paterson. If the plods had Raz, Paterson could get hold of him. He could find out which way Maya and the lads were headed.

I stood on the doorstep while I called Paterson's number. Looked about. No sign of Mossie's Honda.

"Azo?" he said when he answered.

"Yeah."

"Raz is nicked. Looks like Maya's gone off with Mossie."

"So you can stop them?"

"We're going to tail them a bit. Rodney too. See where they lead us."

"If they find out Maya's with you, she's dead."

"She's quite a girl. She's sent me Raz's email login and a load of his bank data. We'll see what else she can dig up from Jihadiland."

"She's not safe."

"She's a big girl."

I growled. "What do you want me to do?"

"Sit tight. We're sending someone round for Raz's fridge."

He rang off.

I went out the front again. Walked down the path and

155

crossed the road. Looked up and down the street. No one around. I headed back to the house. Stepped towards the kerb behind this white van. Something blocked my view.

Bang.

I was face-up in the gutter. My nose was bleeding. The back door of the van was open. Someone was hoisting me up by the armpits. I opened my mouth to yell but something clipped the back of my head and took my voice away. My brain dropped into the black.

Chapter Thirty-One

I went somewhere new in my dreams this time. God knows
how I got there. I was a boy slave on a pirate ship. They had
me running up the mast fixing sails and then going down
under deck and there it turned into a steamship and they shut
me in this sweaty engine room scraping the salt skeg off the
boiler with a stick. It started as a kind of rake in my hand then
it turned into a snooker cue. They called me up on deck to
meet the skipper. And there he was at last. My dad. His eye
sockets were sunken, dark and squishy like two scoops of
chocolate ice cream. A daft pirate hat on his head. He yelled at
me and raised a whip over his shoulder and some other twat
behind me was tearing my shirt off so I'd take my lashes, and
just then my mind swam up out of the syrup.

A spot of light poked through one eyelid. I couldn't move
my mouth but I started to see. A bulb on the ceiling. The
ceiling was red.

I shut out the light. Rested my eyes. My brain. Drifted off
again. The pirates never came back, but the spots of light did.
My head lolled to one side.

I was lying on the floor. My eyelids crackled open.

Some pokey little broom cupboard I was in. There was a
telly flickering in the corner. Someone was sat there gaming
with his back to me. Just a blurry shape next to the flashing
screen.

My neck and back were stiff from lying on the floor. I
wriggled and rolled onto my side. Then onto my belly. My
cheek touched grains. Some kind of cheap thin matting.

I couldn't see the feller and the screen anymore. I was face
down, my head pointing away from him. I saw the wall ahead.
Red paint on steel. Twinkles of light on it from the telly and
the yellow glow from the light bulb.

My arms and legs started to wake up. I was still too groggy
to push myself up sitting. I juddered back over onto my back

and peered down to the corner. I made a scuffle as I moved but the feller stayed staring at his screen, clicking at the handset. What was he playing? Bit of Battlefield it sounded like.

I slackened my neck and looked at the ceiling. The bulb there, rigged to a bracket. White lead running through hooks and out through some little gap in the metal side just behind his armchair.

I twisted my neck sideways and peered at the feller. He sat there clicking away at his Xbox. Dark red hair and freckly neck he had. I couldn't see his face.

I rolled onto my side again. My ribs hurt. I sucked in air through my teeth. Got my hands under my chest and pushed myself up a few inches. My arms ached but I did it. Then onto my knees. Creaked to my feet. Turned and stepped towards him.

I stopped to let my head settle. I was breathing heavily. I coughed and found my voice.

"'Ey," I said. "'Ey, lad."

He leaned forward and smegged at the handset with his thumbs for a couple more seconds. He sighed and paused it.

He tossed it to the floor and turned to look at me. Youngish feller with a square jaw. His neck and back dead straight. He frowned. Then he raised his eyebrows and grinned.

"Hey, buddy," he said. "How's it goin'?"

Eh? Yank. I'd never met one in the flesh. Seen a lot on the telly, fighting and shagging and running up and down buildings. I'd always liked them that way. Tough, honest, randy. Now here was a real one.

"Milk and two sugars," I said.

"Come again?"

"In my tea. Or are you just going to sit there looking pretty?"

He frowned again.

"You feeling alright, buddy?"

"Shite."

He narrowed his eyes a bit like he didn't understand. Then he grinned again. "You mean 'shit'? Yeah. That happens."

"Fuck's all this?"

He frowned and said nothing.

"I need a piss," I said.

"Bucket's behind you, bro'."

"Fuck off."

I lurched to my feet and made a move for what I guessed was the door. The bit where wire from the bulb went through a crack. I'd got two steps towards it when his palm touched my chest.

"Hold on, buddy. No bathroom trips. Not yet."

"Gerroff us, yer quiff."

I parried him and tried to keep going. His hand came back. Faster, higher. Clenched. Bang into my throat.

I dropped to my knees spitting and choking.

"First we talk," he said.

Took me a bit to stop gagging.

"Where am I, then?" I whispered.

"Where do you think?" he said. Not in a sarky way. More like he was trying to get inside my head.

I coughed and looked around me, on my hands and knees. "Your granddad's shed?"

"Something like that."

"Where's he keep his strimmer?"

He looked lost for a sec, then smiled and cracked his knuckles. He stepped back a couple of paces. I sank back onto my arse on the floor. I was out of shape alright.

He went to his armchair and shifted it around to face away from the telly. He sat down and looked at me.

"I've been waiting to talk to you, Azo."

"Want some cheats?" I pointed at the screen. He glanced at it, then looked back at me without smiling.

"I got them already."

"You're hard work, you, aren't you? Go on then. Where am I?"

"You're everywhere and nowhere, Azo. You're inside a dry goods container on board a Philippines-flagged, Lebanese-owned, Hong Kong-chartered cargo ship."

I'd been wondering about that wobbly feeling under my legs. I'd put it down to being out cold so long. How long had I been out?

"Blimey," I said. "You get all sorts docking in Liverpool."

"We're not in Liverpool, Azo. You were brought here by airplane. We're in the Indian Ocean."

It was me doing all the asking so far, but I had this feeling that was going to change. I clicked into Paterson-spy-scum training mode. Made sure I didn't let my shock show.

"You the skipper?" I said.

"Huh? No. I'm a passenger. I'm CIA."

"You can't fuck with me then," I said. "Yanks and Brits. We're on the same side."

"You're not, though."

"Eh."

"A Brit."

"Fuck off."

He paused for a minute. "Where do you think you're from, Azo?"

I pushed myself away sliding on my arse. My back touched the wall at the far end from him. He still hadn't let me have a seat. Or a piss. Or a glass of water.

"Right where you snatched me from," I said.

"Liverpool? Wrong."

"You think I'm lying?"

"No. If you were, I'd be hurting you right now. You can't lie if you don't know the truth."

"You know something I don't?"

"Many things."

"Go 'ead then, smartarse. Where am I from?"

He licked his lips.

"North of here," he said. "Place called Iraq."

"Fuck off."

"For real."

"You've got me mixed up with the guy from the chippie."

He leaned over in his armchair and picked up something from the floor. He stood up and brought it over to me. This orange wallet file. He opened it and peeled out a sheet of paper. Thin and shiny like a chip wrapper. Old and yellow and covered in squiggly black print.

He held it out to me and pointed to one of the squiggles.

"Hami Beshat. Born: Umm Qasr, January 16, 1990."

I took the sheet from his hand.

"Hami," I said. "What's that?"

"That's you, buddy."

I snorted. "You're off your head."

He wasn't though, was he. And something inside me knew it.

I was back on Southport pier. I could see my dad there like always, his muzzy and daft grin. But now for once I could hear him talking as well. I knew his voice. Like it had been whispering away in the back of my mind all those years and someone had just turned the sound up. Or it had been calling from far off and had just got nearer.

"Hami," it said. "Cam on, Hami. Cam on. Big man, Hami. Good man."

It had been playing on a loop underwater in my head. Now they'd dredged it up.

The Yank took the paper back and read from it. "Father: Ali Beshat. Interpreter. Mother: Karen Coke. Nurse."

I felt myself trembling. I wasn't ready. But you never are. No matter how tough you think you are.

"My dad?"

He'd stopped his smartarse act. He was looking at me all soppy-eyed now, like he cared.

"How's the CIA know about my dad?"

He got up, walked to a corner and fetched another chair. Plastic green garden kind. Somewhere to plonk my arse at last. He placed it facing his comfy one. I sat on it with my back hunched. I waited for him to speak.

He let himself sink back into his armchair. He kept his eyes on mine.

"You look like him," he said.

"How the..."

He shushed me with a frown and a raised finger.

"We're watching him," he said. "We watch a lot of folks round here. Only he's not like most folks. We looked into his background. That's how we found out about you, Hami."

"Azo."

He shook his head.

"It's written on my driving licence," I said. "What have you got? Some snotrag with foreign writing on?"

"Paper trail, buddy." He held up the folder. "We got docs here going way further back than your driving test. You. Your dad. Your mum. Iraq in ninety-one."

I knew what had happened there. One of them wars they go on about. I knew my mum had been a nurse for some goody group. I never knew that was where she'd been.

I was feeling queasy but I made myself speak.

"How'd I end up in Liverpool then?" I said it like I still didn't believe him. But I could tell he'd have a good answer to that.

"Duh? Your mom and dad took you there. Dangerous in Iraq in the nineties. She married him and took you both home with her."

"Don't tell me. You got all that on paper?"

He patted the file.

"Why did he fuck off then?"

He sniffed and blinked. "This is where it gets hard, Hami."

"Azo."

"Whatever. They kicked him out of the UK."

I felt sicker. "Why?"

"Eeh... He was dodgy. Full of hate. Dangerous friends. They don't like folks who tick those boxes."

"His job. On that form. He spoke English?"

"Right. Clever man, your dad. Too clever. He thought he could play both sides."

"Eh?"

"He wasn't just helping us. He was part of the axis of evil all along. He was well-trained. Tough. They sent him back there and cut him loose. Lately, he's been in Syria."

I saw myself from outside. Stood up in the air and looked down at me sitting there in that scabby metal box. A right mess I looked.

"Are you working for Paterson?" I heard myself say.

"Who?"

"Let me speak to him."

162

"Who we talking about?"

"Paterson. British intel. He's the one running me."

"*Running* you? What are you, a half-marathon?"

"I'm an asset, you bell-end."

He snorted.

"I don't look like much," I said. "But my mum's well proud of me."

He looked lost for a sec. Then he smirked. Then he frowned like he was listening at last. He heaved himself up out of his armchair and walked out, jinking the wire and clanging the metal shut behind him.

It was locked when I got to it. I grabbed at it, then yanked my hand away. A leccy charge. It nipped my fingertips and whipped up my arm. I yelled and jumped and fell back on my arse.

I took a piss in the bucket and waited.

He was gone so long I ended up lying down on the matting again. Wasn't the comfiest spot, but I dozed off. It was knackering being in my head lately.

When I opened my eyes again, the feller was still gone. Someone else had joined me. When I lifted my head from the floor, I saw it sitting in the corner by the opening, looking at me. A black Alsatian with yellow eyes.

I rolled onto my side and pushed myself up sitting. The dog twitched and growled but stayed where it was. I pushed myself backwards away from it, to the far end. I leaned my back against the metal and waited.

Ten minutes later, the feller clanged in through the door again. He handed me a bottle of water. He stepped back and looked down at me.

"So I looked up this Paterson," he said. "No one's heard of him."

"No one who?"

"You Britskies share everything with us."

"So?"

"So either you're full of shit, Hami, or our Britsky chums are hiding things from us. Which would be bad."

"And it's not bad snatching one of us off the street and

flying him to Shitistan?"

"Like I said, we share everything."

I ground my teeth. So someone on my own side had signed off on this. Paterson always said he worked in the shadows, but this was taking the piss.

"Your leaders gave you up, Hami. Don't sweat it. You're not the first."

"Find Paterson. He'll tell you. I'm doing good work."

"Told you, buddy. If your Paterson is real, he's a ghost and we got an issue. If he's not, then you're bullshitting me, and we got an issue. Either way, we can't help you."

"So they've handed me over to you. What for? If you don't even know I work for Paterson, I'm nothing to you. I've got fuck all else going for me."

"Wrong, buddy. You got your poppa."

I was never top of the class, but I was quick enough to see something was up here. Was Paterson dodgy? I knew from my training those Yanks were up our arses. Well if we were sharing everything, then Paterson should know where I was. He should be out to bat for me. Not letting them snatch me and bully me about my dad. Unless… oh, fuck me. Unless he knew about my dad an' all.

"Tell me more about him," I said.

He clicked his tongue. The dog jumped up and padded towards me. I hunched up but didn't budge. It stopped in front of me, growled and fixed me with its yellow eyes.

The feller came over and stood behind it.

"No, buddy," he said. "You tell me about him."

"Eh? I don't know him." I was angry now. "What's wrong with you? You said you know who I am. Then you'll know I've not seen him since I was four. You're welcome."

The feller frowned and said nothing.

I turned to the dog. "Fuck off, scrote," I said to it.

It barked and lunged. Its two front paws landed on my chest. I was about to gob it but it got its front teeth round my left ear. It held them there, not breaking the skin, just tugging. Hot yok and breath all down the side of my face. If I wriggled it'd bite in.

The feller knelt down on my right side and talked to my free ear.

"He doesn't like people lying."

"I fuc… "

He yelled over me.

"Before you bullshit me anymore, Hami, look the doggy in the eyes and think."

I did it for a minute. Didn't help me sort my thoughts out. He went on.

"Your dad left Syria a week ago. He'd dropped off our grid but we're pretty sure he's headed your way. We want to know where to find him."

"I've never… "

He shushed me again. The dog growled.

"We know about you and Raz, Hami."

"So what?"

"So we know you're with Raz, and we know Raz knows the same people your dad knows. We know you're the link between them. Now you're our link to them too."

I just stared at him. He must have been in a hurry, because when I didn't speak, he took it the wrong way. He thought I was being hard. He grunted at the dog. It tightened its jaw. My head filled with its growling. My ear was burning.

I must have passed out because when I opened my eyes I was lying on my side on the floor and he was at the far end, stepping out through the opening. The dog followed. Its tail vanished and the door clanged shut.

I was on my own again. I dozed. The lights stayed on.

The songs started.

I don't know anything about music, me, but I know what I don't like. Most of all when I'm trying to sleep. All kinds of gash he was playing. Hard smelly crap and techno and stuff off the radio. Rihanna. Shining bright like a diamond. I knew that one at least. Too loud though. My brain was trying to shut down but it couldn't. The light got brighter. I squeezed my eyes shut but the lids were all back-lit.

The noise was right inside my head.

No clue how long it all went on. Next thing I remember I

was sitting up against the wall again and the feller was crouching in front of me holding out a donut.

I stuffed it in my gob and chewed, snorting air in and out through my nose. The dog was sat next to him, watching me. I ran out of strength to chew and just sat there with the donut gumming up my gob. He handed me a paper cup. Foamy white coffee. I held it to my mouth and glugged it down.

The songs had stopped. My head was ringing. Everything looked slow and far away. The feller's voice came through.

"Hey, Hami. Where's your poppa?"

"Wish I knew, mate," I said.

He went out. The dog stayed. The music came back on. Diamonds in the sky.

Chapter Thirty-Two

"Jeez, you're a tough one, buddy."

He was sitting at my side sipping Pepsi from a bottle.

"I don't know nothing." First words I'd said in a few days. I'd just got my voice back after all that yelling. He'd had a doc look at me and brought in a camp bed so I could have a real lie down.

"Not knowing nothing, huh. That must be nice. So you really don't know where your poppa is? Jeez. You almost got me giving up here."

"Almost?"

"Mmyeah."

"I'm no use to you."

"Wrong, buddy."

He reached out and squeezed my shoulder.

"I gotta tell you. I freaked out when I got that you were telling the truth," he said. "But then I thought about it, and I said to myself, what the hell. Whether you know your dad or not, you're still the best guy to lead us to him."

"How's that?"

"Simple, buddy. We drop you back in Liverpool. He's on his way there. So you'll find him. Or more likely, he'll find you."

I laughed, if you could call it that. My lips curled up and my chest poffed in and out. Snapshots of Southport pier flashed through my head. I saw the Iranian ice-cream man outside our old school. Heard the cheesy chimes of his van. Heard the kids singing in the playground. I saw Frank shaking his head and rubbing his eyes when I asked him about my dad. I saw Paterson sitting with a crooked grin as he nosed through my files on his laptop. Heard myself asking him what he knew; heard his snotty drawl in reply. He was shaking his head an' all. Then I saw Raz, his spongy cheeks full of Monster Munch, nodding as he heard my sob story, his bitter grin like he understood.

167

Last I saw the man himself. My dad, grinning as he stood on the pier, gob trailing from his muzzy. My lungs flapped quicker. My dry laugh got harder and rounder and rolled into a scream.

The Yank wasn't getting much sense out of me. He left it a day or two before he came back.

He sat on one of the placky chairs with the dog next to him. I was on my camp bed with my back to the metal wall.

"So. You're going back to Liverpool to find your dad. You're gonna find out what he's planning. And you're going to set him and Raz both up for some of your Britsky boys to snatch in the act. Then they'll be handed over to us."

I wheezed. "You daft bastard. How do you know I'll not just nick off as soon as you cut me loose?"

"You're smarter than that, Azo. We snatched you off the street. We could do it again. Or maybe not you. Maybe Maya."

"You know where she is?"

He nodded. "You do good, maybe I'll tell you."

"You reckon I'd screw over my own dad for some bird?"

"True, that's a gamble," he said. "So maybe not just Maya, then. Maybe Ali too."

Chapter Thirty-Three

They flew me back. I think. Dropped me off with a bag on my head. I pulled it off and I was at the roundabout by the Spar in Litherland. Just like that. Evening. It had got chilly while I was away. Start of autumn.

I was aching all over from that workout in the shipping container. I zipped my hoodie up and felt in the pockets. The Nokia was there. Someone had charged it.

I stood in a doorway next to the chippie. Paterson answered after two rings.

"Ah. The runaway slave."

All chirpy, taking the piss. He paused and I heard him sipping something. I pictured him in his sitting room with one of them massive bulbs of brandy. A record player with Mozart on and some leathery milf unzipping his cords.

I heard him swallow. "What's up?" he said.

"Checking in," I said.

"You've not called in three weeks."

"I've not been near a phone all this time. I left the country."

He chuckled to himself.

"I thought you might have skipped, Azo. So where are you? Ibiza?"

"I'm back in Liverpool. And I've got some goodies on Raz. So take your cock out of your ear and listen."

"Pop," he said. "It's out."

"Feller called Beshat. Raz has been stocking up weapons for him. Now he's coming over here."

"Mm."

"Yeah, *mm*. They said he's my dad."

He was quiet for a sec.

"Who told you this?" he said at last.

I sank to my arse on the pavement. Thought I was going to start crying but nothing came out. I was all dried up inside. I just shuddered and sniffed.

169

"Azo, where are you?" he said. "Stay there."

I dozed off against Paterson's shoulder as we drove. When I came round it was dark. We'd pulled up in a car park somewhere.

I told him all about the Yank. I wasn't big enough to play both sides.

"Do you know about my dad?" I said.

He sighed and lit me a ciggie. He nodded.

"How come them Yanks knew about him?" I said. "How come they got hold of me?"

"I'm sorry, lad. That was out of my hands."

"I thought them and us were bezzie mates. I told the feller I was with you. He didn't give a toss."

"We share everything with our US cousins," Paterson said.

"Everything but me."

"What makes you so boss?"

"Do you think anything would stop us spying on the Yanks if we thought we could get away with it?"

Took me a sec to get my head round that. I'd not been sleeping well.

"You're not spying on Yanks. You're spying on Raz."

"I'm spying on lots of people."

"Well so am I now. You're sharing me with the Yanks. Jealous?"

He smiled and shook his head. "I rather like it," he said. "It feels naughty."

"You ponce."

He chuckled and slapped my shoulder.

"What about this Beshat then?" I said. "Is he my dad?"

He smiled. "Don't be scared, lad. Let him come. There's work to do. Raz is out and about. I made sure he got cut loose so I could keep an eye on him."

"You heard from Maya?"

He nodded. "Smart girl."

"Where is she?"

"On her way home from Syria with Rodney and the lads."

"Here?"

"I'll let you know when she's landed."

"Where am I going now?"

"Back to the house."

"You blagging me?"

"No, sir."

"Raz there?"

"Not right now. He's lying low. The house is empty. We went through it looking for Raz's little fridge. No sign. You're going to track it down."

He gave me some sleeping pills and a wad of cash and dropped me off back at the roundabout. I still had my key. The Yank had given me back all the stuff from my pockets.

I walked round to the house and let myself in.

Raz's room was locked. I snooped around the rest of the place. No one. Nothing. I climbed up to my attic. Still the same sheets on the bed. Everything as when I'd left. I climbed out the skylight, scrambled down the roof and checked the gutter.

Maya had left the biscuit tin there. Placky bag with a few pinches of skunk still in. A few Rizlies left and two old crinkly Regals. I skinned up and smoked it.

Same old view over the roof tops. Dark trees and winking streetlights. Same old Liverpool sounds. Swooshing cars and sirens far off.

It started to spit with rain. I sucked the last of the spliff and flicked the roach into the back garden. I put the Nokia in the biscuit tin and hid it in the gutter. I crawled back through the skylight and into bed and drifted off to the sound of the falling rain.

Chapter Thirty-Four

My dad came to me again in my head. He was wearing shorts and socks and a basketball vest, camo-coloured. A rifle over one shoulder. One of them belts of bullets on the other. Those chocolate ice-cream holes for eyes. He talked to me, and it was Frank's voice that came out, his rough Scouse bark.

I tried to put my arms round him. It was like hugging barbed wire. His bullets scratched me. I stood off and looked down at my arms. There were bullets in them, showing through under the skin like splinters and moving around like maggots, burrowing up and down through my flesh.

I looked up at my dad and asked him if he'd put one of them in Paterson. He reached out and stroked my cheek. Prodded my nose with his fingers, kneading it all out of shape. He opened his mouth again to speak, but I never heard him.

My eyelids crackled open. It was light. My nose was twitching.

There was a smell. Smoky. Toasty. Meaty.

Something was cooking.

I sat up with a jerk and looked around. Half thought I'd see a cup of tea on the bedside table, but not this time. I listened out for sounds from downstairs. Nothing. Just that smell. Must have been coming out of the vent at the back and in through the skylight. My attic was straight up from the kitchen.

I pulled my trackie bottoms on and crept down the ladder. Stood on the landing and listened again. Heard the fuzzle of the telly from downstairs.

I peered down through the banisters. The back-room door was shut but I could hear the telly clearer now. The rattle of a saucepan from the kitchen.

I crept downstairs.

I opened the living room door. All like it used to be. The telly was on but no one was watching it. The kitchen door was open. I went on through.

Some feller.

He was stood there at the stove with his back to me, stirring something in a pan.

I felt like I knew him, even from the back. Thick-set with hunched shoulders. Grey anorak, grey hair. A white skull cap on his head.

A carton of juice on the table. A gun next to it. Glock. One of the chairs was pulled out. A Klashni stood propped against it, the stock resting on the floor.

My foot creaked in the doorway. He turned his head. Chubby face, he had. White beard.

I knew him. Where from?

"Morning mate," he said. Scouser. "Beans?"

He took two plates out of a cupboard and laid them on the table. A pair of slices popped out of the toaster. He laid them on the plates and tipped beans on top, scraping the clingy sauce out of the pan. He sat down and pointed me to a chair with his spoon.

"I've seen you," I said.

I didn't sit down. He handed me a plate and fork.

"You have," he said. "Last time, you had a right cob on."

"Sounds like me."

"Outside The Grace it was."

I stared at him.

He'd been watching me outside Leanne's that day. Then later as I headed to the pub. My last day of freedom. I'd seen him getting off the bus.

"Oh, yeah," I said. "I thought you was a dodgy old sod."

"I know you did," he told me. "I was on your side though."

"You were following me?"

He nodded and grinned, shovelling beans in his gob.

"I lost your trail that night," he said. "One minute you was out and about. Next you was gone."

I put the fork in my mouth. The sweet sauce clung on my tongue as the beans went down.

"Go 'ead then," I said. "What do you want?"

He wiped sauce off his beard and smiled at me as he chewed. That grin. It had made me want to gob him that first day. When I was all het up about Leanne.

"Your dad sent me."

This sound in my head. Like birds flapping. That old balloon of sicky terror swelled in my stomach. I felt like flobbing my beans up.

All these years I'd wanted to get closer to my dad. Now I was nearly there, it felt like getting closer to death.

"I haven't got a dad," I whispered.

"You have, Hami," he said. "You need him and you know it. And he needs you."

I tried to calm the trembling in my arms and legs. Tried to play the part.

"Needs me? That's a laugh."

"Maybe. But he's not scared to say it. He's got plans, your dad. Needs good lads around him. He sent me because he wanted to see you."

"Who says he can trust me?"

"That's what I said. He's old-school, your dad. He reckoned he could smack your arse into line if he needed to."

"He sounds like a dickhead. Where is he?"

He didn't answer. He finished his beans and put the plate in the sink with the pan. I stood there rocking on my heels while he washed up. He came and sat down again.

"So you're with the anti-terror bizzies now," he said. Calm as you like. "How did that happen?"

"Am I fuck. I'm here to *do* bizzies."

"Oh. Right," he said. He widened his eyes and pouted.

"I am," I said. "Pass me that gun and I'll show you."

"So tell me, Hami. Who told you where to come looking?"

"What do you mean? I live here."

"Right. That's why your dad was coming."

"Eh?"

"He was all set to see you. He's been in Liberia. Finishing up the scummy work so Raz doesn't have to. Now he's here. Risky that, for a man like him. But here's the thing: he wanted to see you. Wanted to get you out of this shithole country before we hit it."

I almost laughed. "Get me out of here? How does he think he'll do that?"

"Same way anyone does anything. On a ship. Forget it though, lad. He'll scrap that once I tell him you're a grass."

"Come here and say that."

I acted tough. But all that head-messing off the Yank had scrambled my brain. I didn't know where all my bullshit was leading me.

"Where have you been?" he said. "Who was that picked you up at the roundabout?"

"One of Raz's mates."

"We know Raz's mates. Don't know any that drives a Merc."

"Does Raz know my dad?" I said.

He didn't answer. He poured juice in a glass, sipped it and licked his lips.

"The pigs brought you here, didn't they?"

I rubbed my eyes. Tried to work out who might know what and whether it would tie me to Paterson.

He didn't give me time to think. He put the glass down and picked up the Glock. I started backing away towards the sitting room.

"You grassy pigdog." He stood up, snapping the slide. "Did you think we'd lead you to him just like that?"

I turned my back on him and stumbled through the doorway.

Bingerly-Bangerly-bong.

The round twatted into my back and hurled me forward. The floorboards rushed up to my face.

I'd had my share of beatings. Been knocked the shit out of. Nose broken, lips split. Jaw and cheekbones bashed till my eyes watered. But it was the first time some twat had shot me.

The floor sucked me in. Comfy enough. Something was tugging me back though. A voice. A thing. Inside. It wouldn't let my mind go. Don't slack off, lad, it said. Drop into the black now, you'll never come out.

I gathered all my strength and lurched up onto my side. I

curled one hand up to my right pec and fingered the hole. Out under the tit the round had gone. Blood? Oh aye. Blood and goo.

I put one hand on the floor and tried to push myself up. Breathed in as I did it. Fireworks of pain all through my chest. Fizzy Dolly Mixtures flashing in my eyes. I fell on my face again.

I heard footsteps on the kitchen lino. Creak of the floorboard in the doorway. Then his hands grabbed my shoulders and rolled me on my back. My chest wrecked as I breathed in again. I hadn't the strength to yell.

I should be playing footie with Ali in the park, I thought. Having tea and beans. Playing darts at The Grace with Frank. Should, should. Had a taste of all that, didn't I. Never lasted.

That old twat's face leaning over me now. His jaw-beard. Muttering to himself. Poking the gun in my eye.

Say what you like about how you're not afraid of anything. It's all bollocks. You never know how you'll take it until it comes. Here lies Azo. Born to trouble. Born to fight and lose, and die on the sitting-room floor.

I wanted to start begging, but I couldn't speak. Felt like I'd lost half my blood. I could hardly blink. A ball of puke clenched in my belly, ready to ram up my throat like a scuzzy fist and choke me.

Something warm on my face. Hello. Tears? Fair enough. No one would blame me for having a bit of a blub now, eh. You'd have cried too. Yes you would. Why? Because it's not fair? Because there's people counting on you? Bollocks to that. It wasn't about Ali anymore. Or Maya. Or Frank. Or my dad. It was all about me. It's a selfish business, dying.

Thin door between alive and dead there was now. Someone was waiting for me on the other side. I could feel him. It. Some kind of god or devil, whatever you call him. Some big black crow with a hungry mouth to peck me up and swallow. I'd seen him in my dreams, far off. I wasn't ready to meet him.

Couldn't hardly breathe now. When I did it wrecked. My eyes went dim. I heard the feller muttering. Then a shot. And another.

I lay there dribbling and oozing into the floor. Let my whole body go limp. Nice and hush like a good boy. Waiting for the end.

I heard the feller trying to say something. Grunting. Then yelling. Shrieking. Louder. Madder. Then two more shots. Much closer than before.

He shut up.

I felt arms under my shoulders. My head lolled onto my chest. More hands on me. Under my ankles, lifting my legs. A door slammed. For a minute I was floating. Then my back touched something soft.

A voice whispered in my ear as my mind slid under.

"Don't worry, Iggle Piggle" it said. "It's time to go!"

Chapter Thirty-Five

One of those long fever dreams. The ones that seem to go on all night and day. It started in The Grace, only it wasn't. The sign over the door said the Hugh Crow. I was drinking there with Frank when a bunch of fellers burst in and grabbed me. They chucked me in the back of a cart, drove me to the docks and put me on a ship.

Some of the time I was up on deck, standing and spinning the wheel. But mostly I was shut up down below, naked on huge wooden shelves with the other slaves. Men and kids and grandmothers chained up all round me, pissing and shitting and dying. Some woman came in and fired brown sugar all over us. It got all under my manacles and melted, sticking them to my legs.

The skipper came down and unchained me. He rolled me back up on deck and made me take the wheel.

I looked ahead over the bow. We were heading up out to sea, mowing down all these little rowing boats that bobbed in front of us. I watched the sharp hull of our slaver carving up the folk in them.

A big squid fizzed up out of the Mersey and thrashed against the hull. The ship listed. I heard a drum and chanting from below deck. The monster thumped its white jelly bollocks against the keel in time with the beat. The skipper jumped overboard. The squid opened and swallowed him.

The chanting and drumming got louder. The slaves were singing. I'd had enough of their racket. Didn't they know we were sinking? I went down and laid into them with a whip. It flashed out of my palm like Spider-Man's web. I lashed them slaves to sloppy bits with it till my arms ached. I roared at them till the waves started lapping round my head.

I blinked and slowly woke up, trembling. The blood was churning and booming in my ears. My right shoulder and chest ached.

Someone held the back of my head in their hand and tipped sugary water in my gob. I swallowed and let it wet my throat, washing the skank and dryness away. Bit of strength. I moved my lips and jaw. Peeled my eyes open.

Dim light. Colours and shapes. Someone was sitting next to me. A big blotch of red. My eyes sharpened. I made out white letters.

Liverpool shirt.

"Welcome back, la'."

"Wool twat," I muttered, as I passed out again.

Raz squeezed my good shoulder. I blinked in the light. Saw the red shirt tucked in his camo belt. Big baggy combats on his legs. I tried to sit up. Wicked sting in my chest.

I eased myself back down. Tried just lifting my head. These two tubes coming out of me. Bloody water in one of them. I coughed. The water moved up and down. A white bandage covered my chest.

My head flopped back down. I twisted it from side to side.

He'd laid me in one of the first-floor bedrooms. The one at the back where Rodney had slept. White walls. Old wooden wardrobe. Peeling paint on the ceiling. Washbasin in one corner.

I looked at the tubes, the bandage, then up at Raz.

"Who's done all this?"

He winked and jerked a thumb towards his own chest.

"Shouldn't I be in the hossie?"

"Doctor in the house, la'. Still got the old magic. You got it through the lung but you're alright. It missed the big pipes."

"What have you done to me?"

"Not much. Flap seal. Chest drain. Dressing. No blood to give you. No surgery for the wound. You'll be feeling woozy for a couple of weeks. You'll want to sit off in bed."

He had a strap round one shoulder. Holster with a handgun under his right arm. A Klashni leaning against the wall by the basin.

I was weak, but not just from the wound. I was cacking myself inside. I wondered how much the feller had told him.

I forced my voice out again. "Where's that dickhead?"

Raz raised his eyebrows. "Uncle Bulgaria? He's gone."

I was on my guard. Or as much as I could be while laid up with a hole through me. He was being too nice.

"Gone?"

Raz looked me straight in the eye. "Tea or coffee?" he said.

"Tea."

He went out and came back with a tray. Pot and glasses. He poured out this hot green brew.

I chuckled. It set the bloody juice bobbing in the chest-tube. A twinge in my chest. But I couldn't help it. It was funny really. Some people would say I'd had a hard life. Not me. Working for Raz's gang? It was just one tea party after another.

He held out a glass. I pushed myself up on one elbow and took it. Put it to my lips and blew on the scalding tea. Sweet minty whiff. I sucked it in through my teeth.

"Gone where?" I said.

He pursed his lips and held up a finger to them. Hush.

"Rest, la'."

He picked up the rifle and went out.

I started to move a bit. My hands. Jaw. Had to be careful not to wriggle around or my chest would sting.

I drifted in and out of sleep. Raz came and went, changing my dressing, giving me jabs for the pain. He took those tubes out after a couple of days when the bleeding in my lung stopped. He brought me ready meals and helped me limp to the bathroom.

I could stand up but my chest felt weak. I still had the dressing on. A few evenings later I was sitting up in bed with this plate of chicken and rice when he came in.

He sat cross-legged against the wardrobe and watched me eating.

"You're ready to be up for good," he said.

I finished the rice, leaned over and plonked the plate on the floor. Big placky bottle of Evian there. I unscrewed the top and swigged from it. Raz looked at me.

"What did he say to you?"

"Eh?"

"In the kitchen."

"Nothing. He just started shooting."

"After you'd both eaten your beans."

He sat there gripping his knees in his fingers and stared hard at me.

"*I*'d been having beans," I said. "He just came in with a Glock."

"So you offered him some?"

"He made me. He was messing with my head, wasn't he? Winding me up before he slotted me. He didn't say nothing. He was waiting for something."

"For me?"

"Maybe."

He stared. Hands-free lie test. Like he had that time when he nearly throttled me on the garden path. That bit about the beans didn't look good, eh. I didn't reckon he believed us.

I slumped back knackered on the pillow. I tried my helpless whingey act. See if it would work like last time.

"I don't know what to tell you, Raz. I don't know what's been going on. I just ducked off and hid. I come back here cos I was starving. I thought the pigs had got you."

He cackled. "Ah! Them pigs," he said. "Your old mate they kept in. Me they let go. Why they do that?"

"They've got nothing on you."

"My arse," Raz said. "They're watching me."

I'd cacked myself with that bit about the beans. Now I calmed down a tad. It sounded like he was more worried about himself.

He lit up a Regal and held it out to me. Not too smart that, in my state, but I had other things to worry about. I took it. Enjoyed the taste. Coughed. Didn't see any smoke coming out of the hole in my chest. I must have been healing.

"What you going to do?" I said.

He lit his own ciggie up. "They think they've got me covered. But they've not got my fridge. We're going to work."

"Where?"

He looked at me. "The hour that the ship comes in," he said.

"You. Me. The lads."

"What you talking about? Ship?"

"We shout from the bow: 'Your days are numbered.'"

"Something's happening down the docks?"

He nodded and winked. "Something coming over on the ally-ally-o. Last bit of the recipe. The other bits are in my fridge."

"So what did that twat with the beard want?"

"He's one of the bunch over from Syria." He slurped the last of his tea down in one. "They think I'm a leaky boat."

He raised his hand and lashed the tea glass across the room. It hit the wall at the foot of my bed and shattered.

He took a deep breath. "They've paid me," he said. "To do a job for them."

"So do it. Show them. I'm here."

"Oh I will, lad. Just one hitch."

He picked up a bit of glass and braced the point of it against his thumb. The soft pad of skin turned white and dimpled.

"There's a scum," he said.

My wound stung.

"Someone's robbed dough from us. Hacked us. That's why that twat come after us."

He fixed his green eyes on me.

"It's She-Ra."

"Eh?"

"She's fucked us over."

"Maya?"

"Princess of Power," he said. "Clever girl. She been in my laptop."

"How do you know?"

He winked. "She's the only one been in my room. She'd made a copy of my key. I found it in her knickers."

I blinked and felt the blood surge to my chest. But I stayed in the part.

"I'll do her for you, Raz," I said. "Where is she?"

I dropped my ciggie in the tea glass. It fizzed out in the wet sugar. I sat up and tried to move my legs. A shock of pain hit my chest. My head swam. I wanted to spew.

Raz squeezed my shoulder.

"At   ease,   la'," he   said. "I   got   plans   for   her."

Chapter Thirty-Six

He left me to doze. I lay there dreaming of ways to get hold of Paterson. I'd stashed the Nokia up in the gutter. I'd have to eat a shitload of spinach to climb up there.

I tried to rest and get my head sorted. By night time I felt ready. I ripped back the bedcover and forced my feet onto the floor. Creaked myself upright.

"Namaste."

My knees buckled. I was back on my arse on the bed. Raz was stood there in the doorway.

"Fighting fit, la'?"

He held out a hand. I gripped it while I stood up again.

"Good timing," he said.

"Now?"

"First thing tomorrow."

I looked at the alarm clock by the bed. It was nearly midnight.

He held my arm while I limped up and down the room. Got the blood pumping round my legs again. After a bit I was standing on my own. My head felt light but my mind was there. I just had a dressing on my chest but Raz had taken the stitches out. My right arm and chest were stiff.

He went out and came back with a duffle bag. He undid the zip and pulled clothes out. One of my old trackies and my blue Fila shirt. He'd had them washed and ironed.

"Have you sewn my socks an' all?"

He grinned. Pulled my trainies from the bag and chucked them to me.

"Dressed and ready, old mate," he said. "Then tea downstairs."

He went out and shut the door.

I pulled on the trackie bottoms and wrestled the shirt on over my head and my achy arms. I was lacing up my trainies when Raz came back.

"Ready, la'?"

"Yeah."

"Come and meet the team."

He took me down to the kitchen. The table was set for tea but there was no one sitting down yet. A pan of spaghetti was bubbling over on the hob. Raz turned the heat down. He stood by the sink and pointed out the window.

Rodney, Casho and Ayax were back. They'd got the mats out of the shed and laid them on the grass.

Casho and Ayax had grizzly black beards now. They looked leaner and fitter than ever. Rodney too. This hard look in his eye that wasn't there before. He had a little goatee, the bell-end. He was ducking and weaving around.

They were wearing combat trousers and Nike and Adidas t-shirts. Trampling on the mats in chunky para boots. Running through some moves. But faster, smoother than before. Casho and Ayax were sparring, hurling wicked punches at each other's faces and knees at their ribs and blocking them. Rodney was dancing round them with a wooden sword in his hand, swooping in with it like he was trying to split their heads open. They dodged and blocked him. He plucked something from his belt and went for Casho with it. The lad locked his eyes on Rodney's and squared up to him, creeping round in a circle, looking for a chance to have him. Rodney flicked and spun the knife in his hand. Not wood this time. Real. A nasty pointy job with a jaggy edge.

Ayax stood and watched them. Rodney lunged. Casho did some footwork, stamped on Rodney's thigh to get him down then chinned him and snatched the knife. He held it to Rodney's throat down on the mat. This mad stare in his eye. He stood back off Rodney. Ayax pulled a pistol from his belt and held it to Rodney's head and they all laughed. Casho gripped Rodney's hand and pulled him up. They shook hands. They hugged.

I turned to Raz. He winked.

"They back from boarding school, la'. All that cricket, what. Stiffens a chap up!"

"And where's Hanzi? He using a gun now an' all?"

"He got his part to play."

"Where?"

Raz didn't answer. I looked out over the garden again. The two brothers were ramming the mats back on the stack in the shed. Rodney was pacing back up the garden. He stopped halfway and kneeled on the grass. Got up and put his palms together. Got down on his knees again.

I turned to Raz again.

"You're joking?"

He winked. "Judge not. He's a holy lad now, our Rodney," he said. "Storing up riches in heaven!"

He spooned the steaming spaghetti out into a big bowl on the kitchen table.

The lads came back through the door one by one and wiped their feet on the mat. I nodded at them. They nodded back. They didn't look at me the same as before. Something judgey in their eyes. I understood. They were holy hard men now. I was just some scally who didn't know where he came from.

Raz handed Rodney a key so he could put the weapons back in the crate. The lads went and washed their hands in the upstairs bathroom. They all came back down and we sat round the table for dinner. Half of the big nasty family back together.

Raz served up the spag-bol.

"Dig in," said Rodney, winking at me. "Last supper, innit."

His voice had got weirder since I'd last seen him. West Indies with a bit of Scouse and Cockney sloshed in.

"How you feeling?" he said to me. "We thought you'd never get up."

I didn't answer. I glanced at Raz. No help. His nose was buried in his bowl.

Apples and pots of yoghurt for afters. Then cups of tea. Rodney sat down in the sitting room on a cushion, muttering prayers to himself.

"Come on, then," I said to Raz. "What's the plan?"

He wiped his lips on his shirt. He said nothing for five minutes. Then he looked at me, nodded and slurped the last of his tea down. He stood and led me into the hall. Rodney got up and followed.

Raz went to the cellar door and unlocked it. He switched on a light inside.

My head felt light. My chest throbbed. I didn't crack up though. For once I wasn't scared he might slot me. He'd just spent weeks nursing me.

There was a line of clothes hooks just inside the cellar door. This yellow overall hanging there. Me and Rodney stood back while Raz took it down and climbed into it. Legs and arms. Then from another hook, this white hood thing over his head and shoulders like some nun. Health mask over his gob. Then goggles. Last of all he snapped on these blue rubber gloves.

"You forgot your dildo," I told him.

He tapped the goggles with his knuckles. The sides of his eyes wrinkled and the mask twitched. He was grinning.

No gimp suits for me and Rodney. Raz beckoned us on down the steps.

I followed with Rodney behind me.

I got to the bottom and looked around. The same shadowy light as last time. The torch was hanging from a hook in the ceiling at the far end. A bed on wheels lay under it.

Someone was lying there.

Raz grabbed the torch and turned the beam onto the bed.

He was laid out in a blue trackie with his eyes closed. He'd sprouted zits since I last saw him.

Raz's voice came out muffled from under his mask.

"Brave Sir Hanzi, ladies and gents," he said.

"He asleep?"

"He's poorly."

I stared at Hanzi. He was breathing heavily.

"What is it?"

"Fever."

"What kind?"

"Bad kind."

"Eh?"

"Tropicky kind," Raz said.

"We should take him to... "

Raz nodded and smirked. I shut up.

"That we will," Raz said. "I take care of Hanzi. I take care of all you lads."

I looked around. There was a table against the wall. Doctor's gear laid out on it. One of them curved steel bowls. Needles lying in it.

He'd brought that fridge thing and plugged it in down there.

Raz turned to a table against the wall and fiddled with the stuff there.

Rodney was sitting cross-legged in a far corner. To my left was a work bench and more kit, spilling out of shopping bags. Clamp, drill, hammers, scissors. Screwdrivers and padlocks and packets of batteries. Bits of belts and straps hanging from nails on the wall there.

Raz saw me looking and walked over.

"Kit," he said.

He unhooked a strap from the wall and dangled it from his hand. A bunch of fat padded belts and pockets. Webbing. He squeezed one of the pouches with his free hand.

"We ram this bad-lad with my naughty putty," he said. "Stitch on charges. A deto. Phone it in. Snap, crackle, pop."

Rodney went over to the alcove. He turned his back to Raz and threaded his arms through gaps in the webbing. He clipped it round his waist and chest and grinned at me.

"Not for me, thanks," I said.

They both laughed. "As you were, la'," Raz said. "Takes training to wear one of these."

I looked at Rodney. "Go 'ead, then," I said. "Do us a favour."

He took it off again.

Raz turned to hang the webbing back on the wall. Rodney strode back over to his corner.

"That shit in the needles," I said. "What's that?"

"The magic potion, la'. Wee Lee nearly had off with the first lot. Good job you slotted him."

I clenched my teeth. "What is it?"

"Gourmet shit. Chokes you with fever. Then you start splatting blood. Takes a while. Hanzi's at the fever stage. That means he's ready to pass it on."

The leccy light bulb twinkled off his goggles.

I felt sick. I felt angry more. I'd done Hanzi once. I'd not let him get used again. Paterson wouldn't let this happen. I'd tell him. He could storm in this house tonight and have Raz and Rodney. All this would be enough to send him down. Guns and bombs, plus whatever Maya had got from hacking him.

Where was Maya, anyway?

Hanzi looked alright. Not a scratch on him. Quiet and still.

"I've given him sleepy dust to calm him," Raz said. "But that fever ain't going to sleep."

I kept my voice steady.

"Hadn't we better keep away?" I said.

Raz walked towards me.

"Get a good night's sleep yourself, la'," he said. "Big day tomorrow."

Rodney stood up and all. The two of them looked at me.

I headed for the steps. Raz nodded at Rodney to follow me. I glanced back at him as I went up. He had a gun in his hand now. A big Smithie.

"Want me to hold your cock for you?" I said.

He looked down at the piece then up at me. "Don't mind my little friend, Az."

"Put it away, or it's going up your arse."

"Raz wants me to keep everything ship-shape."

"That used to be my job."

"I'm trained now. I been in the field."

"Shagging sheep?"

He frowned and tried to stare me out. "Evil words, brother," he said.

"I'm not your brother."

"Too bad for you."

"Put it away."

He stared in my eyes and raised the gun, pointing it upwards. Shook his head. I looked beyond him. Raz had his back turned and was fiddling with something on the table. He turned to face me with a Klashni in his hands.

"Go to bed, la'," he whispered.

"Please?"

He raised the rifle to his shoulder. Aiming it right at my

head. He strode towards me.

I stood my ground. Held his gaze. When he got close, he switched the Klashni round. Swung the butt and smashed it across my face.

I went down, gasping, squirting from the nose.

"You grassy little jiz," Raz said.

"Fuck off," I gasped.

He squatted on his heels and cocked his head at me.

"They nicked my Russian sailor lad."

"Course they did, you daft bastard. He was walking round a port with smuggled shit in his bag."

"Then he gave it to you. You was the only one who knew about him. So you're in it with her."

Rodney hauled me up from behind. He held me with an arm round my neck, facing Raz.

"Do us, then!" I yelled. "What are you waiting for? You not got the bollocks?"

Raz closed in and poked his Klashni in my chest.

"Oh, I can't do you now, la'," he said. "We're waiting for you to go live."

"Eh?"

"For your fever to start."

He turned and went to the table. Pulled a syringe from the bowl. Brought it over to me.

"Liberia's finest," he said. "Shaken, not stirred."

"Bollocks. No one gets that here."

"They do now. The Manc had off with some of it. So your dad's come over on the jolly boat. He brought a load more."

I clawed at Rodney's arm, wriggling and flinching as Raz leaned in.

"Hush, baby boo. I won't stick this in you," he said. "I did that already. Three days ago. While you were schweeping."

My arse, I told myself. He's off his head. He's blagging. I felt alright. Or not. I was still all rough with that hole in my chest. If a fever started, not sure how long it'd take me to spot it.

Raz pried my fingers away from Rodney's arm. He yanked my left wrist down and pointed to the flexy bit inside the elbow. Tiny red hole there.

"Takes a few days for the fever start. Then you're ready to pass it on. Any time now."

He mimed pumping his thumb down on the needle. "Good night, schweet pwince."

I snarled. Rodney prodded the muzzle of his gun in my cheek. I had blood dripping down from my nose over my lip. I spat it at Raz, flecking red dots on his goggles.

He grinned. He swabbed the goggles with the thumb of his glove and made like he was sucking it through the mask.

"The others have got it lurgy too," he said. "Tomorrow they go   walkabout."

Chapter Thirty-Seven

Rodney stuck the Smithie in my back and rammed me with it all the way up two flights of stairs. Kicked me up the arse as he shoved me back into his old bedroom and turned the key.

I rattled the door handle. Twat. I heard the floorboards creak outside on the landing as he sat down on guard.

No need to wait for the bug to start giving me the runs, eh. I was shitting myself already. Nothing but dreno keeping me standing. God knew how long that would last.

I breathed. Tried to calm myself down. Didn't work. I was panicking.

I went to the sash window and heaved it open. Looked out over the garden, all dark green and quiet. I glanced up above my head. A few feet of brick then a gutter. Above it, the little flat bit at the foot of the attic roof. Too high to climb in my state. I'd fall and cripple myself.

It went quiet inside. Dark outside. Just this night light on the wall of the house. The air was warm and still.

I was lost. Finished. I sat slumped over the windowsill. Hours went by. Passing out and coming round again. Waiting for my strength to come back or my heart to stop beating. Waiting for my brain to shut down. It wouldn't. Something kept tugging me back.

I didn't know how much time had gone by. My eyes opened. I smelt something.

I hauled myself up and sat on the windowsill with my legs inside the room. Leaned out with my back to the garden and strained my neck back to try and see up onto the roof beyond the gutter.

Nothing. Any further and I'd be arse over tit and break my neck. I listened. Nothing.

That smell again.

I saw something coming from the roof above. A wisp of smoke,

I called out.

A face popped into view over the gutter.

She stuck the spliff in her gob. Narrowed her eyes and peered down at me as she tugged.

That white vest she always slept in.

"You off your pills?"

She nodded.

"I was coming for you," I said.

Daft, that sounded. Even more so from a divvy locked in a bedroom, leaning out of a window. But you couldn't call it a lie. I'd not stopped thinking about her. Just had a long to-do list.

She blew out a lungful with a sigh.

"Come for me?" she said. "What for?"

"I said I'd look after you."

She bowed her head lower and muttered something.

"Can't hear," I said.

She flicked her hair back and looked at me, still leaning over the gutter. She was crying.

"Like you did my mum," she hissed. "Like you did Lee!"

"We've got to get hold of Paterson," I said. "Where's my phone?"

She flicked the hot roach down, right into my eye. I nearly toppled backwards. Held onto the window frame just in time. The spliff fell into the garden, spilling sparks in the dusk.

I looked back up at her. She'd turned her head to one side. She'd heard something. I ducked back in my room and listened too. A noise out on the landing. Steps shuffling around.

When I leaned back out of the window, she was gone.

My body was aching. I shivered. My head felt light. I slapped myself in the face.

I managed to rip a leg off the bed and started trying to batter the door handle and lock to bits with it. Wasn't happening. I stopped and grabbed the alarm clock by the bed. Ten to seven.

I heard Maya coming down the ladder from the attic. Rodney and Raz calling from below. I heard her steps cross the landing and stop.

A key turned in my bedroom door.

When I got out onto the landing it was empty. Footsteps clattered down in the hall and the front door slammed. I heard a noise from the other bedroom. This throaty groaning wail like a trapped dog.

Hanzi.

He was there on the bed. Awake now. His eyes met mine. They were all sunk in, His face was white.

He was sweating. Sobbing.

"Alright, lad," I said. "You be alright now." I'm a boss liar, me.

I went to the window. Dragged it wide open and stuck my head out.

Raz's and Mossie's cars were pulled up to the kerb by the garden gate. I made out shapes in the back of the Honda. Casho and Ayax. Mossie at the wheel. Rodney was on the pavement by the Astra. He was bending over, pushing someone else into the back of it. Maya, in a baggy black robe and headscarf.

She ducked into the car without looking back.

Rodney got in the driver's seat. He shut the door and revved it up.

I pelted down the stairs three at a time. Hall, front door. Locked. I booted it. The frosted glass gave way in the frame, shattered and fell out in bits. The gaps weren't big enough to climb through. I glimpsed the Honda peeling away from the kerb. The Astra with Rodney and Maya was gone.

I turned round, puffing and swearing. I was starting to sweat.

"Alright, Hanzi lad. You're alright. I get help."

I looked up in the attic room and the gutter for the Nokia but it was gone. Just Maya's biscuit tin lying open. A bag with a last pinch of skunk. I pocketed it. I'd be needing some painkiller.

No other phone in the house. I'd have to run and find one. I legged back downstairs, calling out to Hanzi the whole time, telling him he'd be alright. Into the back room. Kitchen. I pulled open the door to the garden. Stepped out, peering round to the side gate.

It all went dark. A stink of paint shot up my nose.

A bag over my head.

Two sets of hands wrenched my arms behind me and hustled me along. I yelled inside the hood. *Stay away*, I tried to yell. *Lurgy!* A lot of good that did.

A car door opened. A hand shoved my head down and pushed me inside. Once I was sat, the hand rammed my head between my legs and held it there, fingers round my neck.

I shivered. The blood was pounding in my ears. I mumbled and wriggled in my seat and the bastard gripped my neck tighter. The car started. We ragged off.

Voices muttered.

We stopped and the car door opened. Hands dragged me out and hustled me along. Up steps. Doors banged open and they thrust me to my knees.

Chapter Thirty-Eight

"We're on the same side," I mumbled.

The bag came off.

A beardy face looked at me. Took me a sec to place him. He looked shocked when he saw my face.

"Eh?"

Ralph. My old trainer from the posh jail. He stood back and dropped the bag on the floor.

I sat up and looked around. Not much to see. Panelled door and peeling yellow wallpaper.

"Where am I?"

"Not far, mate. Safe house off Linacre Lane."

"What time is it?"

"Eight."

"You've got to get after them."

"Don't worry, mate. We're all over it."

"But they're... "

"We've followed Mossie and Casho and Ayax to Lime Street. They've bought their tickets."

"Trains?"

"Ayax to Birmingham. Casho to London. Mossie to Leeds. We'll see where they lead us. They're going to lay this cell wide open."

"But they're... "

"Don't worry, lad. None of them was wearing a vest."

"You daft sods. He's jabbed them full of lurgy."

"Eh?"

"It's what he had in his fridge. He's jabbed it in me too."

He took a step back.

I held onto the floor and tried to calm the shivers.

"Where's Hanzi?" I said.

"On his way to hossie."

"Were they wearing yellow suits?"

"Eh?"

"The medics. He'll be coughing it all over them."

He stared at me. He got on his phone. He acted like it was all in a day's work but I could tell he was crapping himself. He walked over to the window and peered out through the curtain as he jabbered away. He looked at me over his shoulder. Hung up his phone and stuck it on his belt.

"We'll grab them," he said. "Fly them to the Royal Free. Seal them off."

"And Maya?"

"Rodney's taken her off somewhere. We're following."

I thought of the baggy robes she was wearing.

"There was a bomb vest," I said. "It was for her."

He looked at me. He got back on his phone.

"You going to get me sealed off and all?" I said when he was done. "Better get yourself looked at too."

"We'll sort you out," he said. "After your big date."

"I've had a wank today already."

"Raz thinks he's getting away. Thanks to Maya, we know how." He pointed the phone at me. "You're going after him."

"Why don't you go? He'll kick my arse."

He reached in a jacket pocket and handed me a shiny new Glock.

"That all I'm getting?"

"Seventeen slugs in there, Az. Plenty."

"Raz has got Bombs. Klashnis."

"David and Goliath, eh?"

I stuck the gun in the back of my trackie bottoms. He took me down to the car. Same old Golf he'd driven when he dropped me off in Tocky that first day.

We bombed down Knowsley Road to the docks.

We stopped by the fence along Crosby Road. Ralph killed the lights. He got out and went to the boot. Took out a roll of carpet. He carried it to the fence and rolled it open over the spikes.

I scrambled up. The prongs were pricking through the carpet. I just made it before they bust into my arse-cheek. I dropped down on the other side.

Ralph pointed into the dock. I turned to look. Shipping

containers stacked three high. Orange carriers zipping around, picking them up and loading them onto the blue gantries that plonked them on the ships.

In between me and the dock there was a scrap of old railway. Then another fence. Not that high. But it had curly-wurly rolls of barbed wire on top.

I turned to Ralph and stared at him through the fence.

"First stack of red containers on the right. There's a feller in a yellow jacket," he said. "He'll point you the way."

"You joking? I'll get nicked."

He grinned and shook his head. "Once you're in the container, it'd take the bizzies months to find you. There's cameras watching the fence. You're a fast runner."

I looked at the barbed wire. Ralph humped the carpet over the first fence till it flopped down on my side. I gathered it up while he drove off.

I nipped across the rails, lobbed the scrap on the barbed coils and scrambled up and over.

No one in sight. I scanned the lines of crates and cars waiting to be loaded on the freighters. A yellow vest popped out at the foot of one of the stacks.

I ran.

He worked a lever at the back of the crate and pulled the door of it open a few inches. He pointed inside and put a finger to his lips. I pulled myself up and kneeled there on the floor.

His face vanished as he shut the door. The rubber seal squeaked. It went dark.

I found a space on one side of the cargo and groped my way around. Stacks of boxes. A narrow gap down the middle of them. I squeezed along through it.

There were air holes somewhere. I could breath, just. But it was stinky hot in there. Or was it the fever?

I stood there in the dark with the smell of petrol and damp sacks. Heard a sound. A dry rustling. Somewhere near me. And again. Lighter than creaking wood. Heavier than dripping oil. Steadier. Real. Alive.

I held my breath and listened.

Laughing, it sounded like. Or crying. Hard to tell. Soft, sobbing, sniggering sound.

A few yards away from me it was, at the back end of the container.

I groped my way along the gap in the dark. Stepped on a pallet. My right foot went through between two planks. I swore and tugged my foot. Wedged tight.

I held my breath and braced my arms against the crates. Yanked away at my right foot, biting my lip with the pain. Trying not to make a sound. I yanked again. Sweating. Praying.

I heard voices outside just as my foot jerked free.

Crack of pain. I bit my lips and steadied myself against the crates. Heart heaving. Head spinning. Lungs leaping. A big yell trying to burst out of me. I choked it down.

The voices died away.

I tiptoed through the gap and round the far end of the stack, head and shoulders first. I couldn't see a thing but I could smell his sweat. Hear his breathing. There was a gap between the last boxes and the back of the cabin. He was there on the floor.

I slipped the Glock out and held it down beside me as I squeezed towards him. I got down on my knees and laid a hand on his shoulder. He lifted an arm and gripped my hand where I was touching him. That sound again from his mouth. Muttering nonsense. Gasping. Blubbing.

He slumped into me and rested his chunky head on my chest, quivering and crying with no sound. Dribbling on my top.

I hauled him upright and slapped him awake. He sighed and shivered.

I grabbed his shoulders and shook him. He wasn't sobbing anymore. The noise had got quicker, higher.

Giggling.

I let him slump back down. He fumbled around. I heard the scratch of a lighter.

The flame flared under his nose and lit his face up. A ciggie in his gob.

I sprang back and pinned my shoulders against the side, cowering as far away from him as I could in the few inches I had.

He blew the smoke towards me and kept the lighter burning. The flicker of it caught the muzzle of his rifle, leaned against the side of the crate. His gold teeth. His beard and shaven head. Earrings. His cheeks were slick with blood. His eye... what was wrong with his eye?

"Them sparks is flying upward!" he said.

His glass eye seemed to look at me in the glow. His other one was gone. Black nothing in the hole.

The flame went out. Just the sweet smell of Regal smoke. He tittered and sobbed in the dark.

"Raz, what happened?"

"Oh, that Beshat," he said. "Closer than the jugular vein!"

"He's here?"

"He's old school, your dad. Likes to settle his own scores. I told him it was you the scum, not me. But it's all the same to him. Caught up with me at the container depot. Taught me a lesson."

"You need help, mate. I'll take you to a doc."

"Witch doc?"

"Eh."

"I'm shipping out, lad. Seaforth containers! They plonk us on that jolly boat any time now."

"Raz, you're blinded."

There was noise outside the container. A truck grinding around out there.

"Little nooky cranny for me under the engine room," Raz was saying. "Hot and cosy. Shipmates hand me butties all the way to Mombasa."

I saw the red rock on the end of his ciggie bobbing up and down in the dark.

"Where's Maya?" I said.

"She why you came, eh?"

"Where?"

"Bomb vest and no knickers! Something for the telly!"

I stuck the Glock where I thought his neck was. I was no

better off than him in that pitch-dark bin.

He shoved me off. I crashed back and landed on my arse. Dropped the Glock. He lunged and groped and got his hands round my neck. Lifted me up like that and shoved me against the boxes. Slammed me a couple of times. Then he eased his grip and let me breathe. He held me still with one hand.

"At ease, la'," he said. "Don't trash your old mate Raz for Maya's sake. She's wrong in the head."

"That why you chose her, eh?"

He shrugged. The sick bastard.

"Well your plan's messed up now, isn't it," I said. "The pigs have got them all."

"Not so, la'. The plan's just taking off."

"Eh?"

"Any pigs come near them lads, they slash themselves up and splat a bullet through their brains. Spray their sicky blood all over."

"So you put a few people in the hossie."

"Few, yeah. Three rush-hour trains? Few dozen. Enough to get folks panicking. Enough to mess up the hossies. Only one unit in the UK for that kind of thing and it ain't big enough. And no one knows how to cure the bastard."

I twitched with rage. Was that it? All my running around for Paterson and he lets this happen?

"What about Maya?" I said. "She can't pass it on if she's blown to bits."

"True enough, la'. It's not about the bug with her. Told you he's old-school, your dad. Hers is just your everyday bomb vest. Rodney'll make sure she gets there. Then they phone it in to set the belt off."

I wriggled. "Where?"

"Hmm, yah, let me check my watch. By now she'll be near the gates of Saint Rock's."

"Eh?"

"It's little Ali's first day of big school, eh?"

Go 'ead, Mr God Mate Lad. Take me now. Nice and quick. I won't tell.

Something clunked on the roof. The carrier-crane was

grabbing us. Gave me a jolt. In a good way. Snapped me out of my whingey daydream. Fear cut through my fever and sparked me up.

Raz slackened his arms a tad when he heard the bump. He wasn't ready for me. I swung my head back and let fly, all the way from the heels to the snap of the neck. Bang. I closed the gap before his arms could straighten. The top of my crown crunched square on his nose.

He was a big one, but Ralph was right. Nothing like a Kirby Kiss to take the legs from under you. Raz crumpled onto his arse.

I jumped on him. I groped around and picked up the Glock. Rammed the muzzle into his neck.

"Where's your phone?" I hissed.

He blew air through his lips, spitting blood. He shrugged and chuckled. I raised the Glock and smashed the butt down on his nose. What was left of it. Nothing seemed to hurt him. He just moaned a bit and cackled to himself.

"Ooh-la la!"

"Where?" I said.

"Ain't got one. They don't work at sea."

I felt the box sway and tilt. We were in the air. They were carrying us to the ship to load us.

I saw myself from the outside. Right daft prick I looked. Hunched over this lummox with a gun, in a box, on a crane. I froze. Raz smirked, spitting out blood.

"Nice girl that, Azo," he said. "Get a move on, you can hold her hand. You can hold Ali's an' all!"

"You daft prick," I said. "You said you'd set her belt off by phoning it in."

"Dead right, la'."

"Then you said you had no phone."

"Not me. Your dad."

My pits were streaming. I dug the gun deeper in his neck.

"Where?"

"Your top pubby-wub."

Where all this shitstorm started.

"I'd hurry, la'. He'll be shipping out an' all before it all goes

202

off."

I shoved him away, fumbled around in the dark and got hold of his rifle. I slung it on my shoulder and limped round the stacks. Groped my way back to the door I'd come in by. No latch on the inside. No catch that I could see. I rattled and banged on it. No good.

A few weeks back I'd been lying staring at a door just like this one, when the Yanks had me laid out.

I put the Klashni to my shoulder and raised the barrel as far as I could in the space. Wriggled back into the gap in the cargo to get another inch or two. Braced my knees against the floor. The container was swaying in the air. I trained the rifle halfway up the door and heard the muzzle clank against it.

I tried to guess where the locking rods were that ran down the door on each side. A few inches out from the rubber seal. Levers on them half way up and the bolts they snapped into.

I stopped. I didn't know how much use Raz's rifle slugs would be on the steel door. Might ricochet back and slot me.

I groped around behind my back. Some kind of wooden bed stood upended there, wrapped in sheeting.

I squirmed around in the space, humping and dragging the bed about. Worked open a gap behind to shelter in. I angled the Klashni over the top of it, pointed it as best I could at the middle of the door.

I took a breath, braced myself against the bed and frigged away at the trigger in the dark, biting my lip at the din and the smoke.

The slugs were useless by themselves. But Raz had the rifle full. At least thirty rounds. I fired them all.

I stepped out from behind the bed and squeezed round into the space, waving the smoke away. The door was still there. I bashed at it with the butt of the rifle in the dark. A spot of light showed near the middle. The metal had buckled. Part of the rubber had snapped out. A blade of daylight cut through.

I dropped the gun, squared my back against the load and hoofed the door till the bolts and levers gave out.

I knelt down and squeezed my head and shoulders through the opening. My throat was dry. My head was spinning. My ears were dead from the din of the shots.

We were twenty yards up and dangling from a gantry. Just a few paces of hard ground from the side of the ship and closing.

I let my legs down into space. Hung on the edge with my hands and dangled. I swung gently. One, two and I let myself drop.

I'd already frigged my ankle getting stuck in that pallet. It twisted again as I hit the ground. My right wrist jarred as I stuck it out to break my fall. I didn't feel the pain yet. I was back on my feet. I whipped the Glock out of my trackies and started limping away.

I was nearly back where I started. Seaforth container dock. The Grace was just across the road.

There were dockers around in their hard hats. They yelled but didn't get close when they saw the gun. I ran through the gaps between the stacks of containers. Out again and through lines of new cars. On towards the back of the depot. Fifty yards from the fence.

The dock bizzies had woken up. They had one car coming along the line of containers. Another heading for the fence.

I made it there first. Ran for the spot where my scrap of carpet was flopped over the barbed wire. I scrambled over as the bizzie car screeched up to the fence.

No time to drag the carpet on with us to the outer one. The one with the three-pronged spikes on top. I left it draped over on the inner fence, ran to the far one and jumped.

I yanked myself up and crouched on top, my arse an inch from the spikes. Shifted on my toes as I braced to spring over. Sparing my bad foot. All the weight on the left. I shivered. The balance was all wrong inside my head. My trainie slipped in the dew on the steel. Spike stabbed right into my arse cheek. Tore through my trackie, gashed into the top of my thigh. I squawked like a fanny. The spike scooped out flesh as I tumbled into the road where the overpass comes down.

I staggered over, dripping blood, to The Grace. Its red bricks and peeling paint. A dim light through the frosted glass. I hobbled in under the corner arch.

Chapter Thirty-Nine

Gibbsy looked at us through his milk-bottle specs like a scared owl as I came through the porch door.

"I've not told him nothing," he said.

I started to turn. I felt a flutter at my back as the Glock slipped out of my waistband.

He stood there with it in his hand.

A snapshot. But old and scuffed now. That same muzzy and grin. Them jokey-around eyes, but wrinkled at the edges. Too friendly to be good. Hard-friendly.

"Hami, man," he said. "Good man, Hami."

He was shorter than me. He looked like some sad old git. This big black padded jacket. Same floppy fringe. Grey in his hair at the sides.

I've gobbed on a bit about my dad, haven't I. Spent all those years wondering about him. But Frank was right. It's hard to know what you're really after. All that time thinking about it, and now I didn't have anything to say.

I stood there panting and just looked at him till he spoke.

"I come a long way to be here," he said.

"To kill kids? What's this then, your tea break?"

"It's not all work, work, work."

I stared at him.

"What do you want?" I said.

He shrugged. Grinned. Sucked his bottom lip. It bunched up his muzzy like in that snapshot.

"You."

I thought of my mum. I felt sad. Mad. I wanted to go home to my bedsit and curl up in my old bunkbed with a tinnie.

"What for?"

He shrugged. "Take you home."

"You took your time."

He took a phone out of his pocket. Black Nokia. He pressed a key and held it out to me.

I didn't take it. I looked at the clock above the Liver Bird mirror. Ten to nine. The front gate at Saint Rock's would be rammed with kids.

"Come on, Hami," he said. "Show me whose side you're on."

You'd have thought I'd have lots to say. Lots to ask. It was what I'd always wanted, eh. Meet my dad. But I didn't know what I felt now. Didn't feel much. Couldn't even feel my arse and my wrist and ankle hurting any more.

I peered at the screen on the phone. He had a number keyed in there, ready to dial. To set Maya off.

I stood there in that gloomy pub, bleeding into the carpet.

"Gibbsy," I said. "Get us a lemon squash?"

Beshat waved the phone under my nose. He brought the gun down from his shoulder to point at my chest. His finger switched off the safety.

"Press the green button, Hami," he said. "Then I'll take you home."

I heard Gibbsy wheezing as he plodded up behind me with the squash. I kept my eyes on Beshat and reached back with my left hand. I couldn't feel my wonky right wrist after that tumble.

It was one of them chunky glass beer mugs like always. Good old Gibbsy. Old school. I felt my fingers slip through the handle as he held it out to me. I tightened them round it. I pumped my right elbow down and swivelled on my good left foot as I swung the glass.

He was a tough bastard, my old dad, but he was slower than me. He knew how to fight in the desert, but I knew how to fight in Bootle. A wicked left hook with a pint tumbler of lemon squash on the end. It knocked through his gun-hand. The knobbly glass smashed into his jaw. He went down.

The phone bounced away under a table.

I knelt down next to him and picked the gun off the doormat.

Chapter Forty

The phone goes. I let it ring out on my pillow. I've got my hands under the bedsheet, skinning up the last of Maya's skunk. My fingers are trembling but I reckon I'll get there.

Raz was wrong about the isolation wards. There's another one they don't tell us about in the news. One for Paterson's boys. It's in the posh jail where Paterson trained me.

I asked the doc if she'd let Ali and Frank in here to see me, if they wear those lurgy spacesuits. I wouldn't cuddle Ali yet. Just wave and say hello. It'd help me get better. I'm feeling weak, but the doc says I can beat it. She said she'd see about Ali and Frank. Won't be long, I reckon. Paterson will have to let me see him. I've done my bit.

I get the thing skinned up, sort of. Got no lighter though, have I.

It rings again.

My dad's phone. What a joke. I wouldn't have kept hold of it only I want to ring Frank. I look at it. Still ringing. Sod it.

I press the green button.

"Good morning, sunshine."

I raise my hand with the phone in. Want to get rid of it now, but there's nowhere to chuck it, is there. I'm inside this lurgy tent so no one touches me.

I never want to hear from this bell-end again. Can't run from him though, eh. I've learned that much.

"So your American friend gave me your dad's phone number," Paterson says. "He's quite a chap."

"The Yank? He said he'd never heard of you."

"He just thought he hadn't. He's here with me now."

"That's handy," I say. "You can go and bum each other."

"There, there."

"I thought you'd have it in for me. You wanted him alive."

"Don't worry about that," Paterson says. "Doing your old man, that took guts. We won't forget it."

"What about the lurgy?" I say. "We didn't stop that. How many people are going to die?"

He clears his throat. "Well *you*'ll be alright, Azo, for one."

"And on the trains?"

"Thanks to you, we snatched them before they could spread it around."

"Happy endings."

"Up to a point."

"Why?"

"No one knows where Maya is."

"She was headed to Saint Rock's."

"Well, she and Rodney vanished when her belt didn't go off."

I grip the phone in my fist like I'm about to lash it away. Look up around me at the see-through curtains.

"We think your dad's lot have her," Paterson says.

"You're meant to be battering them over there so they don't come over here."

"We're all fighting the good fight, Azo. You, me, Maya. We've got to fight it together."

"Well we've messed up here."

"Someone usually does. You did your bit though. Hanzi's alive. We've sealed him off like you. We've some goodies we'll be testing on you both."

I stare out through the curtain at the blurry white walls.

"That lad, that first night," I say. "What did they tell his folks? Why I never went down for it?"

"Oh, Azo. Don't worry. That lad from The Grace? He didn't die."

I speak again. My voice comes from far away.

"That morning in the cells," I say. "You told me I killed him."

"I lied, Azo. I needed to make you sign my papers."

"I killed his mate though, didn't I?" I say. "I killed Lee."

"You did your job, lad. You did well."

"And now I'm going to see my boy."

He clears his throat.

"When I'm better," I say. "He and Frank will be wondering

where I am."

"Best if they don't know."

I feel tears pricking up in my nose.

"You said I could see him if I did the job," I say.

"Job's not finished."

"I was a good lad before I met you," I told him.

"Forget who you were before, son," he said. "You're one of mine now."

THE END

Acknowledgements

Thanks for your precious help and support:

Sabine Beausseron, Jamie Coleman, D.J. Connell, Helen Corner-Bryant, The Curries, R Curtis Venture, Jennifer Donnelly, Mark Fitzpatrick, Pirate Irwin, Richard Lloyd Parry, The Lloyd Parrys, Kelly Macnamara, Sarah Morris, David O'Reilly, Ad Parkes, Dan Peck, Patrick Preston, Nat Segnit, Jonathan Sissons

Azo Coke will return soon in HOUSE OF BIRDS

rolandlp@hotmail.com

Printed in Poland
by Amazon Fulfillment
Poland Sp. z o.o., Wrocław